ZOMBIE BOY 2

ESCAPE TO COBB ISLAND

K.S. HALL

SUMMER MOON PRESS

This book is dedicated to my brother Stephen Hintze. Hang in there, like Aiden, you've got this! You are loved.

THE BLACK HELICOPTER banked sharply left as Aiden Winters peered through the window. Sunlight dipped low on the horizon, and darkness approached, the sky turning a burnished golden-purple. They had flown for several hours and had finally begun to descend.

As they circled the small island, lush groves of palm trees mixed with native pines dotted the landscape below. Several seaside hotels, painted shades of white and aqua blue, hugged the shoreline. Usually he would have been excited about a beach getaway. Not today. Aiden shifted uncomfortably in his seat, a sick feeling low in his stomach. Even though he was infected with the virus turning everyone into a zombie, he hadn't turned completely, and so the government wanted to study him. Everyone seemed to think he held the cure to the XR-30 virus that had overtaken the world.

Aiden swallowed past the lump in his throat. He'd only found out a few days ago that his mom had been infected too. She was a zombie now. He glanced at his dad sitting beside him. It seemed like a miracle that he'd found his dad at the CDC. Aiden had his new friends, James and Cecily to thank for that.

"Headquarters are just beyond that ridge," Admiral Walker shouted above the noise of the rotors. He was the military leader who had rescued Aiden. "Cobb Island is the perfect spot for our research. Although isolated on all sides by the ocean, with only coast guard access from Maryland, the island is large enough to house a sufficient military presence," he said, grabbing onto a safety strap as the chopper banked again. "We've cleared the island of all infected, and only a handful of civilians remain. It's taken considerable effort, but we've managed to assemble a team of scientists from Japan and Israel. More will be arriving soon. You're a welcome addition Dr. Winters and, of course, Aiden," he said, glancing his way.

Aiden squirmed, glancing down at his hands in his lap. They were so pale the blood vessels looked almost black against his skin. He had the hands of a zombie. What if he disappointed everyone? What would happen to him then? He swallowed the lump in his throat and looked out the chopper's window.

A grand two-story home with white wood siding and black shutters came into view. The setting sun glistened off the green metal roof and turned the windows a glittering gold. The house was surrounded on three sides by a wide, covered porch. Pine trees, flower gardens, and acres of manicured lawn spread out on all sides. This place looked too perfect, like the virus wouldn't dare touch it and had skipped right on by.

Soldiers stood guard at every corner of the house. Dressed in black from head to toe, a machine gun in their hands, they scanned the area for any possible threat. Obviously, they weren't taking any chances. Aiden stiffened as the chopper gently touched down, and the pilot switched off the engine.

Aiden glanced down at his ripped pants and dirty shirt and shook as fear rose up in his throat. He looked terrible, just like the dead that roamed the world now. Dad must have felt him shaking because he reached over and unfastened Aiden's seat belt.

"I'm here with you, Aiden. Don't worry, son," he said, patting his arm. He peered closely at Aiden and then smiled. "Everything will be all right."

The whine of the engine died down, and several soldiers rushed to open the door for the Admiral. Two more soldiers and a man in a white lab coat ran underneath the slowing blades to open the other door for Aiden. They carried a stretcher with them. He didn't want to get on that thing, but dad nodded encouragingly, so he allowed himself to be hauled like a wounded warrior across the field and into the house.

Well, he'd thought he was going to the big house, but instead they carried him across the wide lawn and down to a boathouse next to a small dock. The boathouse reflected off the water, the sound of the ocean lapping against the shore. A row boat, tied to the dock, bobbed up and down with the waves. Aiden relaxed a bit. Dad was with him now.

There were thick metal bars on the windows, which suddenly turned the charming boathouse into a prison cell. Maybe this wasn't such a great place after all.

Dad noticed the bars too and whispered, "It's for your protection too, Aiden."

Maybe, Aiden thought, grimacing, but it seemed like they expected him to turn and attack. *That would totally suck.*

The soldiers opened the door and carried him inside the dim room. It was filled with all kinds of equipment on shiny carts. They transferred him to a cot at the far end of the room. One of the men reached into a cabinet and pulled out leather restraints.

Dad flipped out.

He'd barely found his dad a few days ago. Dad had thought Aiden was dead from the virus, and Aiden had thought the same thing about him. His dad was super protective now.

"There's no need for those," Dad said, scowling. "Aiden's not dangerous. I'll stay with him."

"We have our orders, sir," the soldier replied nervously, fiddling with the straps.

"Well, go tell Admiral Walker I won't allow it," Dad said, crossing his arms.

The soldiers nodded quickly and rushed from the room. The lock clicked behind them.

Dad sighed, looking around the boathouse.

"This can't be the main lab. It's missing some key equipment. It must be up in the main house," he said, talking to himself while he walked around the room.

Aiden wiggled on the cot until he was sitting up. Even with all the lab equipment, there were hints of the room's former use. A green kayak was propped in the corner with paddles lying next to it. Several life vests hung from a hook in the opposite corner. A sign on the wall read: "Life's better by the beach."

Dad sat on a stool next to a table, his shoulders hunched. He had dark circles under his eyes. It had been a long, tiring day for everyone. It was hard to believe that only twenty-four hours ago he'd been kidnapped and thought he'd never see his dad or any of his friends again.

There was a knock on the door, and Admiral Walker entered. He had three men with him.

One man was older, with the brown skin of the Middle East, and the other man was younger and Asian. The third one was a tall black man with glasses. They all wore white lab coats.

"I'm sorry, Dr. Winters," the Admiral said. "The

President's on the island. We wanted him sequestered at NORAD with the rest of the government, but he insisted on being present when Aiden was brought in. Naturally, the Secret Service is very cautious. Once I explained the situation, they agreed you could be Aiden's guard, but for everyone's safety, they'd like to keep the door locked."

Dad hesitated then relaxed and nodded.

"May I introduce Dr. Basheer from India and Dr. Takahashi from Japan. And this is Dr. Benton, head of research on Cobb Island."

The men shook hands with Dad. The scientists eyed Aiden curiously, walking towards him and stopping a few feet from the cot. Dr. Basheer shook his head, his eyes wide.

"If I didn't know better, Aiden, I would swear you were a *turned* zombie. I can understand people's fears," he said in English, although he spoke with a slight Indian accent.

"Give them some time to get used to Aiden, all right," Admiral Walker said, looking at Aiden. He opened a closet and motioned to a cot and more blankets. "You can stay here with Aiden. It's not the most comfortable accommodations, Dr. Winters, but at least you'll be close to your son. We'll start blood samples tonight. President Harrison would like to meet you both in the morning. After that, we'll jump right into the research."

"Of course," Dad said and walked with the men

to the door, but this time Dad stepped outside with them, closing the door behind him.

Aiden could hear the murmur of voices as they talked. He knew he would be poked and prodded with needles and who knows what else, but it would all be worth it if they found the cure. Plus, it was going to be pretty cool to meet the President. James and Cecily would have loved that.

Thinking about his friends, he managed a crooked smile. He hoped they would be okay at the CDC and wondered when he would see them again.

He sighed, lying back down on the cot. Even though he was locked inside the room, a small sense of peace and safety flowed over him. Maybe this would all work out, after all. As he gazed out of the window, there was just enough moonlight to make out the gentle waves lapping softly against the dock.

JAMES HADLEY MARCHED down the corridor, shifting the heavy box of supplies from one arm to the other. John Winters, Aiden's uncle and head of security at the Center for Disease Control, had enlisted his help delivering supplies to the new family that had arrived this morning. With the virus spreading rapidly, the town of Richmond, Virginia was becoming a dangerous place. In the week since James, Mom, Cecily, and Ella had taken refuge at the CDC, several more families had arrived, also seeking shelter.

Aiden, the zombie boy they'd met a few weeks ago, had been taken to a remote location. Mom said the scientists were going to study him and try to find the cure. He hoped Aiden would be all right. It would be really amazing if Aiden really was the cure.

James knocked softly on the door at the end of the dim hallway. He was surprised when his sister, Cecily, opened it and held the door wide. Two small boys, about four or five years old played on the floor with toy trucks, while an anxious-looking woman held a baby. A man stood up from a chair and crossed to James, taking the box from his arms and setting it on a table.

"I'm Derrick Ellis. This is my wife, Victoria, our boys Liam and Jonah, and our baby, Rose. Thank you for bringing these supplies," he said, lifting a package of diapers from the box. Derrick went on. "We're so relieved that we made it here safely. It's been crazy out there. We ran out of food a few days ago, and it was too dangerous to look for more. I was worried about what would become of my family if something happened to me."

James nodded uncomfortably. He knew how lucky they were to be at the CDC. There were many frightened people in Richmond. He didn't know how long it would take for the scientists to create a vaccine, but he hoped it would be soon.

"We're glad you made it here," James said, shifting from one foot to the other.

Cecily pulled a small teddy bear from the box and handed it to the baby. "I'd better go finish my chores. I'll see you later, okay?" she said to the boys, patting the small head of the youngest one. "I'll come back around noon and show you to the cafeteria."

As soon as they left the room, James asked, "What were you doing in there?"

They entered the stairwell, heading to the third floor. Mom was in the cafeteria and wanted help making the many loaves of bread needed for the next few days. With so many people living at the CDC now, feeding everyone was a full time job.

"Mom asked me to help with the little boys. They were scared and crying when they got here," Cecily said.

James nodded, slightly out of breath as they marched up the stairs to the third floor.

Yesterday, Dan Powell, a former military man who had helped them get Aiden to the CDC, had warned James to expect more survivors to show up. James worried about Aiden a lot. Not just because he might be the cure to this awful virus but because Aiden was his friend.

When they entered the cafeteria's kitchen, the smell of beef stew simmering on the stove made his stomach growl, and he was suddenly eager for his lunch. Mom stood at the counter, kneading dough and shaping it into rolls for dinner. He didn't know what everyone would have done without his mom. She was good at cutting hair and organization, but she was also the best cook—well, the only cook really —at the CDC.

Cecily ran to Mom and hugged her waist then popped a piece of carrot from the cutting board into her mouth.

"Can I help? I can chop the carrots," Cecily said.

"Sure, but be careful. The knife is sharp," Mom said, eyeing her cautiously. As soon as she was sure Cecily wasn't going to cut off her finger, Mom covered the dough to let it rise and crossed to the large pantry, taking stock of the supplies. She frowned and nibbled on her thumb nail.

"What's wrong, Mom?" James asked, coming to stand beside her.

"We're running low on supplies," she said, rubbing her forehead. "We need flour, oil, and sugar, among other things. With more people arriving every day, the food won't last long."

Dan and John entered the kitchen in time to hear Mom's words.

"John and I were planning go into the city tonight for a supply run, Patty," Dan said, resting his hand comfortingly on Mom's shoulder. "If you'll make a list of the necessary items, we'll see what we can find."

Mom nodded and flopped down onto a chair to write the list.

"I'll round up a few volunteers for tonight," John said, nodding, and left the room.

"Can I go too? Please, Mom?" James asked. "With all the men going, you know

I'll be safe."

Mom frowned, and he could tell she was about to say no.

"I'll tell you what," Dan said. "How about James watches from the van and helps stack the supplies in the back? He's old enough to help out, and I'll look after him. We'll be back before it gets too dark."

"I guess, as long as he's with you," Mom said, glancing up at Dan. She trusted Dan. He liked him too.

Yes! James thought, excited. He hated being left out and figured there might be something special he could bring back for his mom's birthday in two days. He really wanted to surprise her with a small gift.

"I'll be careful, Mom. I promise," he said. Anticipation shot through him. Tonight he would see for himself what was really happening in Richmond.

[3]

AIDEN WATCHED the dark reddish-black liquid drip
from his arm, slowly filling the small glass tube. The
lab technician had taken so much blood this week
Aiden was surprised he had any left. He sighed,
staring up at the ceiling from his cot. Dad had warned
him last night that the scientists would be taking tissue
samples next. He'd spent hours pacing around the
boathouse, wondering exactly what that meant, but
the lab tech had only swabbed his mouth for samples
of his saliva. It wasn't as bad as he'd thought. At least
so far. It sucked that he couldn't talk to his dad and
ask him all the questions swirling around in his head.

Jack, a middle-aged nurse with a shiny, bald head
and a full beard, removed the needle from his arm.
He applied gauze and a large bandage over the area
then pulled off his latex gloves.

"All finished for today, Aiden. Try to rest," Jack

said. He gathered up the tubes filled with his blood and left the boathouse.

A soldier stood guard outside the front door and waved briefly to Aiden before closing the door again and locking it from the outside. Everyone was cautious about him but nice too. They'd fed him every day through IVs, and he'd even been able to sip some water. Dad was encouraged and said he showed signs of improvement.

Was he really getting better? He hoped so. He wanted a real future, not one as a zombie.

Aiden gazed at the ceiling fan, counting the blades as they circled slowly overhead. It barely stirred the warm air in the room. Summer was not the best time to be cooped up inside the boathouse. He longed to jump in the ocean and cool off. He was afraid he might sink though.

There was a knock on the door, and a key turned in the lock. He hoped it wasn't someone coming to take more blood. He was beginning to hate needles.

The door swung open, and President Harrison stood in the doorway. He knew it was the President from photographs he'd seen, although he never thought he'd meet him in person. Dad was beside him, and he ushered the President into the room.

Aiden sat up clumsily. He couldn't believe it. He was in the same room with The President of the United States!

"Aiden, I'm President Harrison. I couldn't wait

any longer and had to meet you. Our team of doctors and scientists are very optimistic. Thank you for being such a brave young man," the President said, his white teeth flashing a smile in his tan face. He didn't come any closer though. "I'll leave you to rest. Keep up the good work, son."

Aiden nodded. He wished James and Cecily were here. They would have loved to meet the President too. There was an awkward silence for a moment as if the President were waiting for a response from Aiden.

"Aiden can't talk just yet, but I'm sure he's very happy to meet you, sir," Dad said finally.

President Harrison nodded, and with a wave, they left the room, closing and locking the door behind them.

Wow. That was cool, Aiden thought, *except the President stayed by the door, like he was afraid he might be attacked or something*.

Aiden sighed and lay back down on the cot. He wished they had stayed longer. The truth was he was tired of being stuck in this room. There was no one to talk to, especially when he couldn't speak anymore. The boathouse had no television or video games to pass the time either. Oh well, he probably couldn't play the games anyway.

A soft tap came from the window behind him, and Aiden turned his head in surprise. A girl peered at him through the bars, her eyes wide. He sat up and stared at her. Who was she? The girl motioned him over to the widow.

Hesitantly, he crossed the wooden floor until he was standing in front of the window. The girl had brown hair pulled back into a ponytail and large green eyes. Freckles danced across her nose. She smiled and put her finger to her lips, indicating she wanted him to be quiet. Did she know who he was and that he couldn't talk? She lifted a notebook up for him to see and began to write. After a moment, she held up the note.

Hi. My name's Ava. Are you Aiden?

He nodded. Who was this girl? He'd never seen her before today. He hadn't known there was another kid on the island. He wondered if she was the only one or if there were more kids around. There was a soft bark, and the girl bent down and picked up a small brown-and-white beagle, a leash in her hand. She must have been walking the dog. It wiggled furiously in her arms as she held it up for him to see. After depositing the animal back down on the ground, she wrote: *That's my dog, Coco. Can you open the window?*

It was cool that she had a dog. He liked dogs, but he'd never had one.

Aiden nodded and studied the window frame. His dad had opened it yesterday to let in some fresh air. He tugged a bit and discovered it wasn't locked. Maybe he could manage it. Using both hands, he pulled until it slid open a few inches. It would be enough to hear what she had to say.

"Oh my gosh, I'm so excited to meet you, Aiden. You're all anyone talks about at the house. Aiden this, Aiden that. Even my dad talks about you, and he's the President! You're totally famous!" Ava whispered in a rush. "Daddy told me I couldn't come near you because of the virus, but that's just dumb. You're the only interesting thing on boring Cobb Island." She sighed dramatically.

Aiden could only stare as she rattled on.

"I told Daddy I was going to walk the dog, but that was really an excuse. I just had to meet you. I mean, we're the same age and everything! I can't imagine how horrible it must be to be a *zombie*," she said, dragging out the word for effect, her eyes huge. "I mean, at least you don't want to eat me." She paused for a second. "Do you?"

Aiden shook his head. Did this girl ever stop talking?

"Good, because if you tried to eat me then I couldn't come see you again. Gosh, I'd hate being stuck in the boathouse all day. Do you like comic books? I have some cool ones if you want to borrow them. I'll sneak them out to you later. It'll be our secret. I better get back before the Secret Service guys come snooping around looking for me. Oh, one more thing." She pulled a cell phone out of her pocket and, turning around, took a selfie with him behind her.

"Perfect. Got to run. See you later, Aiden," she said. With a wave, she marched off, pulling Coco behind her.

Even though cell phone service hadn't been working for a while, Ava must have found a way to charge her phone. He liked the idea of having Ava as a friend. He'd been lonely, thinking he was the only kid on the island. He wasn't much into comic books, but he was so bored maybe he'd read them anyway.

Just then a soldier appeared next to Ava and glared in Aiden's direction. Aiden stepped back from the window.

"Excuse me, Miss Harrison," the soldier said. "You need to stay away from the boathouse."

"I was just getting Coco," she said quickly. "I'm coming."

They turned and hurried away. Ava peeked over her shoulder and waved at Aiden. A smile stretched across his pale face. Somehow, after the whirlwind that was Ava, he didn't feel so alone anymore.

[4]

JAMES SAT in the back of the large, white van as John maneuvered it around a few abandoned cars. They drove past an overturned motorcycle, its back wheel bent at an awkward angle, making it useless. Dan rode shotgun, his rifle across his lap. Toby, a lab tech with blond dreadlocks down his back, took the seat next to James. They'd seen several zombies in the last few blocks, but Dan didn't seem too worried.

James wasn't worried either. Excitement shot through him. He was finally out from behind the walls for a few minutes, and he didn't want to waste time being scared.

"Where are we going?" he asked, leaning between the seats to look at Dan.

"The grocery stores were cleaned out over a month ago. We're heading to an area of Richmond where the homes are surrounded by several acres of land. These types of homes usually had gardens. They might have some supplies and canned goods left," Dan answered.

They turned onto a road with a large sign that read, "Pinedale Acres." The houses were surrounded by fields and tall trees. John slowed the van as they passed the first house. It didn't look good. The windows were broken, and the front door was open. It looked dark and abandoned. A lone shoe lay on the driveway, like someone had lost it in their rush to escape. They passed several more homes in similar condition before they came to a long, circular driveway at the end of the street.

John turned the van onto the pavement, slowly inching forward. The house was a red brick, one story rambler surrounded by rows of towering pine trees. The grass was long and overgrown, but there were flowers blooming in the window boxes. That was kind of strange.

"Do you think someone's in the house?" John asked Dan as he turned off the van. They sat in silence, the only sound the ticking of the cooling engine. James thought the house was probably empty, but then a curtain twitched in the front window.

"I'm going to look around," Dan said, opening the passenger door and climbing out, his rifle ready at his side.

The front door of the house burst open, and an

old woman stepped onto the porch, a shotgun raised to her shoulder.

"Hold it right there," she called, pointing the gun at Dan.

It was almost funny. The woman was at least eighty, with white hair and gold-rimmed glasses. She was dressed in purple pants and a matching purple-and-gold floral top. She cocked the gun to show she meant business, and Dan raised his hands in the air.

"We come in peace, ma'am," Dan said quickly. "We're from the CDC and are in the area looking for survivors. Are you all right out here? Is there anything we can do for you?"

The woman glanced towards the van, and John waved. When she spotted the CDC logo on the side of the vehicle, she seemed to relax a bit and slowly lowered the gun. "Well, I have to admit I'm glad to see you. I've had to run off a few varmints who were up to no good. They just wanted to steal what little I had left."

"Sorry to hear that, ma'am. I'll admit we're looking for supplies, but we certainly aren't here to steal from you. I'm Dan, and that's John in the driver's seat. James is in the back seat with Toby."

Dan motioned for us to get out of the van. Once we were all on the porch, the woman lit a kerosene lamp by an old wooden rocking chair. She gazed at the men cautiously, but her face softened when she spied James standing beside Toby.

"I'm Wilma Jenkins. Why don't you all come on in the house. I've got some sweet tea and cookies in the kitchen. It's getting too dark out here to see properly anyway."

"Thank you, ma'am," Dan said as they entered the front room.

It reminded James of his grandma's house. A blue sofa sat along one wall next to a large, brown recliner. Pictures of children and grandchildren hung on the wall above an old upright piano. Knitting needles and several balls of yarn peeked out of a basket next to the sofa.

"Come on back to the kitchen and have a seat at the table. I don't care if it is the end of the world. I've still got my manners," Wilma said, ushering the group into the kitchen. After setting the lantern on the counter, she placed a plate of cookies on the table and gestured for everyone to sit down. James took a big bite of a chocolate chip cookie and closed his eyes at the delicious goodness. He couldn't help the small groan that escaped his mouth.

"Are you alone out here, Wilma?" John asked, after swallowing a mouthful of cookie and wiping his mouth with a napkin.

"I'm a widow," she said. "My husband, Hank, God rest his soul, has been gone for eight years now. We were blessed with two sons. My oldest, Philip, works in New York at that fancy Wall Street place. He's always so busy. I don't see much of him. Mark, my youngest, lives down in Florida with his wife and my three grandchildren. I haven't heard from either one of them since this whole thing started." Her hands shook slightly as she gestured for James to have another cookie.

He took the offered treat. Wilma was a nice lady. He didn't like the idea of her being all alone out here.

Dan must have felt the same way because he said, "I don't think it's safe for you to be out here by yourself, Wilma. We were in the area searching for supplies to take back to the CDC, or we may not have found you. There are several families living with us now, and we could really use your help. Would you consider coming back with us?"

Wilma refilled James's cup and carefully set the pitcher of tea down on the table and sighed. "That's probably for the best," she said, dropping into the chair next to Toby. "I hate to admit it, but I've been quite frightened all by myself out here. Could I take a few of my things with me?" she asked. Dan nodded, and she added, "I have a kitchen full of food that I'd hate to leave behind. You'd best take that with you too."

Wilma sat for a moment, staring at the ticking clock on the wall, then suddenly slapped her leg and stood turning to Dan.

"Like my daddy always said, 'Don't let the grass grow under your feet.'" She began clearing the table.

She insisted on washing and stashing the dishes

neatly away while Dan, John, and Toby loaded the van with the contents of her pantry. James helped her carry a suitcase to her bedroom and sat in a chair watching while she packed her clothes. A pretty silver hand mirror on the dresser caught his attention, and he moved over to examine it. He wished he had something like this to give his mom for her birthday.

"Do you want to take this also?" James asked, picking up the mirror and touching the delicate roses embossed along the handle.

"Oh, no. I don't have room in my suitcase, and at my age, I don't think I want to look in too many mirrors." Wilma said with a wink, laughing softly

Gathering his courage, James asked, "Could I have it, ma'am? Tomorrow is my mom's birthday, and I don't have a present to give her."

"Well now, isn't that the sweetest thing? Of course you can have it. What a nice boy you are!" she exclaimed, patting his shoulder.

His cheeks grew warm, and he looked at his shoes. He hadn't been so nice lately, what with sneaking off with Aiden and then hiding in the Chinook. Maybe this birthday gift would smooth things over a little bit with his mom.

Wilma finished packing and zipped her suitcase. It was heavy, but James lugged it to the front room.

It took about an hour to load the van. Wilma had a lot of stuff. Toby and James loaded the food while John stood lookout, his rifle close by. Dan was at the back of the van, stacking everything neatly. He whistled appreciatively as a box filled with canned peaches, apples, and apricots joined the rest of the supplies. After her suitcase was safely stowed in the back, James climbed in the van while Dan helped Wilma into the front seat next to John. They had hoped to find supplies, but they'd gotten more than they'd planned on. They had Grandma Wilma now.

[5]

AIDEN'S bare feet slapped the sand as he trudged along the beach. After being isolated in the boathouse for a week, Dad had made arrangements for Aiden to get a little fresh air and exercise. The soldiers followed them but kept their distance, watching from the trees. That was okay. He was happy just being outside with his dad. The sun was warm, but the ocean waves felt wonderfully cool as they lapped against his feet.

"Look at this," Dad called, stooping down to peer at something that had washed up on the beach. A small pink-and-white jellyfish lay in the sand, its tentacles barley moving. Dad grabbed a stick of driftwood and carefully lifted the creature, depositing it gently back in the surf.

Aiden felt just like that jellyfish, left to the mercy of whatever fate had in store for him. He had no idea how all this virus stuff would turn out. Maybe he was destined to stay a zombie forever.

Dad walked ahead, wading into the waves that broke against his calves. A seagull glided on the breeze overhead, finally landing near the tree line. Aiden wished he was as free as that bird and could fly away from all of this. A glint of sunlight reflected off of something on the sand beneath the bird. He moved closer to get a better look. Picking up the shiny object, he brushed off the sand from a small pocket knife. The handle was made of cheap plastic, its camouflage pattern half gone and the blade rusty. It still looked in pretty good shape though. Aiden slipped it into his pocket. The knife was pretty cool, and maybe James would like it.

Looking out across the expanse of ocean, he could just make out the shore of Maryland. It was only a few hours away by boat, but from where he stood, it might as well be another world. He wondered what was happening back in Richmond and if his friends were okay.

"Aiden, come on," Dad called, gesturing.

Aiden trudged through the sand to stand by his dad.

"How are you holding up? Are you tired?"

Aiden glanced at his dad and shrugged. He wasn't feeling sick anymore so that was an improvement, but he was tired of being alone in the boathouse. Dad was working with the scientists most days, leaving Aiden by himself. If only his friends were here, it wouldn't be so bad. Dad had helped him shower and put on clean clothes this morning. It seemed like he was doing better, but he didn't think Dad could give him what he really wanted: his old life back.

"Dr. Winters, Aiden!" a voice yelled from behind them.

They turned to see Dr. Benton trudging through the sand towards them, his white lab coat flapping in the breeze.

When he reached them, he rubbed his hands together, smiling. "I have some good news. One of the test mice responded favorably to the newest vaccine. We're hopeful that we have found what we've been looking for."

"That's great news!" Dad exclaimed. "What strain of vaccine was it? I was wondering about J-459."

"Yes, that's exactly the one." Dr. Benton nodded. "I'm sorry to cut your time here short, but we need Aiden in the lab right away."

"Of course," Dad said, taking Aiden's arm and leading him back towards the boathouse.

Did this mean they were close to finding the cure? Aiden smiled as a bit of happiness flowed through him. He sure hoped so. He was tired of all the needles. Plus he wondered if he'd run out of blood one day soon.

"I know this is hard, but you're doing great, Aiden. You've been very cooperative, and somehow we'll beat this thing. We *will* find the cure. We *have* to find it," Dad exclaimed, almost as if he said it enough times then it had to happen.

Aiden limped beside him, hoping with all his heart that his dad was right. It sucked being stuck as a zombie, but if he could save other people, maybe it might have been worth it. Maybe.

6

THE AFTERNOON SUN beat down on James as he walked beside the brick wall surrounding the CDC. His sneakers crunched the dead grass, kicking up dust. He'd been patrolling the grounds with Dan twice a day since they arrived, and he enjoyed the exercise. It was the perfect excuse to get some fresh air and take a break from Mom's watchful eyes.

She had eased up a bit since they'd brought Wilma back with them from patrol though. She loved her birthday gift and used the mirror when she gave haircuts. She was happier than he'd seen her since the beginning of the virus outbreak. James was glad about that. Mom had been so worried about them. She still worried about Aiden though. He wondered how he was doing and hoped the scientists were getting closer to find a way to end this virus for good.

"Did you hear from Dr. Winters today?" James

asked Dan. The CDC used a high-frequency ham radio to communicate with Admiral Walker and Dr. Winters on Cobb Island.

Although things around the CDC had been uneventful the last few days, James still felt uneasy. After all, zombies roamed the streets just beyond the walls.

"Sorry, James. I wish I had good news for you. The last communication I had was a week ago. They're still conducting tests but have found no cure yet. I know it's hard to be patient, but they're working day and night," Dan said, pulling a bandana from his pants pocket and wiped the sweat off his face. Max, Dan's German Shepard, trotted beside them, his tongue hanging out of his mouth as he panted in the heat. It was almost August, and today had been a scorcher, reaching one hundred degrees.

"I hope Aiden's okay," James said. What kind of tests were the scientists doing? He wished he could talk to Aiden on the radio, but that would be impossible, as Aiden couldn't speak.

They marched along the wall until they reached the back gate. Three white vans were parked behind the building, next to the maintenance shed. John kept the vehicles filled with extra cans of gas and a B-O-B, or bug out bag, for every person. The B-O-B was a backpack with enough water, food and supplies for seventy-two hours.

Two more families had taken refuge here yesterday. Counting Grandma Wilma and the lab technicians Ben and Toby, Amy, Jeff, the nurses, Dan, John, and James's family, there were twenty-five people living at the CDC.

"Have you heard anything from Ashland's safe zone?" James asked.

"Not much. John has been in contact with them and said Chen is in charge," Dan said. Chen had been Frank's right-hand man and had taken over the Ashland safe zone when Frank had been killed. James felt bad that his ex-friend Parker had lost his dad to the zombies, but Frank had done some bad things and almost ruined everything.

James stopped walking and glanced around. Something about this particular morning bothered him. It was too quiet. The birds had stopped chirping. No dogs barked in the distant. Not even a squirrel scurried through the tree branches. The sun beat down on his neck, but the wind had stopped, as if it was holding its breathe. A sense of foreboding pulsed through the air.

Dan looked around and slowly lowered his gun, poised to shoot. He crossed to the metal gate at the entrance, which was secured with a thick steel chain, and peered through the crack.

"I don't like it," Dan mumbled. "Something doesn't feel right."

He walked back to James and cocked his head as if listening to something in the distance. James heard it then too, and his stomach dropped. A low, deep rumble echoed down the street. Dan grabbed James's arm, motioning for him to follow. They ran quickly to the safety of the building.

As soon as the door shut behind them, Dan said, "Let's head to the roof and get a better look."

Cecily appeared in a doorway and gasped when she saw James's and Dan's troubled faces.

"What's happening? Where are you going?" she asked as they ran past her.

"Come on," James said, pulling her with them.

They raced up the stairwell to the top floor. Running to the other end of the building, they climbed the last flight of stairs to the roof. His heart pounded, and fear gripped his throat. He hoped the low buzzing noise wasn't what he thought it was.

Zombies. And by the sound they made, he guessed there were a lot of them.

James walked carefully to the edge of the roof. The hum was louder now, as the undead drew closer and distant moans sounded above the din. Cecily cried out and pointed to the end of the road.

A mass of infected moved in the direction of the CDC. Would the gate keep them out? James didn't think so. With that many zombies pressing against it trying to get inside, he didn't think the gate would hold for long. It was hard to tell how many infected were out there. It looked like hundreds, maybe even thousands. Certainly more than they could fight off.

Dan swore softly. "Alert Patty, Ella, and the rest of the families in the basement corridor that a zombie horde is approaching. I'll get John, Amy, Ben, and Toby from the labs. Meet at the vans in three minutes. We have to leave now!"

Cecily and James ran.

The next few minutes were a blur of chaos as everyone dashed about, gathering a few precious belongings and racing to the waiting vans.

Cecily and James piled inside with Mom. Ella climbed onto her lap clutching Mopsy, her stuffed bunny, tightly to her chest. After loading a couple of large boxes filled with emergency food and gear into the back of the van, Dan climbed into the driver's seat. Toby took the passenger's seat. Max sat between them on the floor, his ears back, growling low in his throat as he sensed the danger around them. Cupcake, Cecily's kitten, meowed softly from a box at her feet. Wilma and Amy, along with Derrick, Vicky, and their kids, climbed into the other van that was parked behind them. They rest of the families climbed into the third van. Within moments, everyone was ready. John opened the back gate and motioned the vehicles through. As soon as the they'd all cleared the gate, he jumped inside the last van.

James turned to look behind them as they drove away. He hated leaving the CDC, but it wasn't safe anymore. He wondered if they would ever be safe again.

The zombies beat on the metal gate with their mangled, infected hands. The moans and screeches reached a frenzy as the zombies spread out, surrounding the building. Sweat trickled down James's back. They had barely made it out in time. A minute more and they would have been trapped.

It was a good thing Dan had made everyone practice an evacuation drill yesterday. He'd assigned spots in the van and stood at the back door of the CDC with a stop watch. The first drill took eight minutes, and he'd said that wasn't fast enough. They'd done it three more times until they finally made it to the vans in four minutes.

"Where are we going?" Ella asked Mom, pulling nervously on Mopsy's ear. Mom hugged her close.

"I assume you have a plan?" Mom asked, leaning over the seat toward Dan.

"I radioed Admiral Walker. We're heading to the Virginia coast to a small town called Mathews. Captain Reynolds will be waiting with a boat to take us to Cobb Island."

James sighed in relief, slumping against the seat. Aiden and Dr. Winters were on Cobb Island. He was going to see Aiden again. Excitement and fear warred within him. Everything would be all right if they could make it to the island.

"How long till we get to the town?" James asked.

"It depends on road conditions or if we run into trouble," Dan said, grimly. "If all goes well, it might be three or four hours. Best to expect a day's trip though. It's already evening, and we might have to stop for the night."

Toby pulled a road map out of the glove box, spreading it across the dashboard.

"Look out," James yelled as a zombie stumbled from behind a parked car right in front of the van.

Dan swerved, missing the infected man and almost running into a telephone pole. His grip tightened on the wheel, his knuckles white. Dan was pretty calm most of the time, but James could tell he was worried. A tense silence filled the vehicle as they continued down the road.

"I promised the Admiral we'd check on the Ashland safe zone and warn them about the danger heading their way," Dan said. "If some of them want to join us, we'll make room for as many as we can. Unfortunately, Cobb Island has limited space, so we can't bring everyone."

James didn't want to stop. He wanted to get to Cobb Island as quickly as possible, but he understood that they had to warn Ashland. The people there would need time to prepare for the horde of zombies heading for them.

He gazed out the window as Dan wove through the streets of Richmond. The maze of wrecked and abandoned cars was like a haunted house at Halloween, with the undead popping out from behind the cars and buildings like grotesque ghouls.

Cecily glanced at him with wide, frightened eyes, watching for his reaction. He tried to look unconcerned and picked up the kitten and placed it on her lap. She smiled slightly and held Cupcake close. Good. She would be distracted by the kitten for a while, and it could take hours, maybe even a day to get to the coast. That was, if they even made it through this crazy, dangerous, infected world.

7

AIDEN WAS ALMOST asleep when the door opened and his dad entered. Grabbing a chair, he moved it next to Aiden's cot and sat down.

"I have some news, Aiden. We've just heard from the CDC in Richmond, and they're on their way here. They're driving to the Virginia coast. The US Coast Guard will pick them up there and bring them to the island. You'll be seeing James and Cecily soon."

Aiden wanted to jump up, shout for joy, and hug his dad, but when he tried to sit up, his head felt dizzy. He was feeling a little weak today from all the blood tests. They'd taken *a lot* of blood.

"Jaa," he croaked and almost fell off the cot.

Did that come from him? The word felt strange as it moved through his throat. He swallowed hard and tried again.

"Jaa... mes," he stuttered, but this time the word was clearer.

He did it. He had just said James! He couldn't believe it. He could talk! Okay, maybe just one word, but it was a start.

Dad stared at him in disbelief.

"Aiden, you spoke!" he cried as he blinked back tears. He bent over and hugged him tight. "Can you say anything else? Will you try, son?"

Aiden peered up at his dad. He really wanted to please him and wished he could tell him everything he had been through and all of the pent-up feelings running through him.

"Da..ad," he finally managed to whisper, his voice hoarse.

Dad's smile lit up the room. He reached out and pulled Aiden close.

"Great job, Aiden," Dad whispered, hugging him tightly. He stepped back, his eyes bright with tears. "I'm going to inform Dr. Benton of your progress right away. He'll be so pleased." Dad patted Aiden on the arm once more and rushed out the door.

Aiden lay back on the cot and sighed. Happiness swelled inside him for the first time in a long while.

Another positive thing was that his hearing had improved in the last few weeks. It was like his hearing was *better* than normal. Even when he was inside the boathouse, he could clearly hear the owls and crickets, the birds chirping and waves as they crashed against the shore. He hadn't told his dad yet though. He didn't know how to say all that anyway. He felt weird enough being a zombie.

He was excited to see his friends, but he was worried too. He'd been on the streets of Richmond and knew how bad things were. The virus was spreading, and it wasn't safe. Something really bad must have happened if the group was leaving the safety of the CDC. He hoped it wouldn't be too long before they made it here. It had taken him and his dad several hours to get to the island by helicopter, and the CDC group was driving. They had to cross the harbor by boat. It could be days before they reached Cobb Island, if they even made it.

Aiden pulled himself upright and stumbled to the window. The morning sun reflected off the ocean waves, and a seagull flew overhead, cawing a greeting. Aiden watched it disappear from sight.

His friends would make it here safely. He wouldn't let himself consider anything else.

He was interrupted from his thoughts by a small bark and footsteps coming his way. Ava was chasing Coco down the hill towards the boathouse. She slowed to a walk as she got closer, picking up the dog and slipping quickly behind the building. He crossed to the back window to meet her.

"Hi, Aiden, I just heard the news, and I came as soon as I could. Admiral Walker says that there's a group from Richmond coming here," Ava whispered excitedly. "I can't tell you how happy I am. I've been the only kid on the island, except for you, of course, and I'm going nuts!" She slid a new comic book through the bars of the window, and it fell onto the pile on the floor. Ava was nice to bring him the books, but between the lab tests and visits from his dad, he hadn't really felt like reading.

"I hope one of the kids is a girl," she said, pulling her phone out of her pocket, and snapped another selfie with Aiden.

He shook his head. *Girls.* What was the obsession with pictures of themselves?

"I have to document everything," Ava said as if she'd heard his thoughts. "Once we get the internet going again, everyone will want to know all about you. You'll be an instant hero."

Ava was the only one he'd seen with a cell phone in months. Although she only used it to take photos she was never without it. He guessed that was a privilege that came from being the President's daughter. Her excitement at the prospect of new friends was contagious, and he was suddenly even more excited to see James and Cecily again. Maybe today would be a good day, after all.

[8]

JAMES STARED OUT THE WINDOW, his forehead pressed against the glass. It was hot inside the vehicle, even though the air conditioning was turned on high. It didn't quite reach him where he sat in the backseat, and beads of sweat trickled down his neck. After a terrifying few minutes escaping Richmond, they'd turned the small caravan towards the Ashland safe zone. Each vehicle was equipped with a two-way radio that Dan used to communicate with the other drivers. Dan glanced anxiously around as he drove, while John and Toby poured over the map and talked about bridges and which route would be the best.

"The quickest way would be I-95, but I doubt that's clear," Toby said. "I suggest Highway 1 as our best option."

Dan nodded, his eyes scanning the road as he drove. Ella was sprawled across Mom's lap while she stroked the little girl's head and listened to the men make plans. Cupcake was curled into a ball on Cecily's lap, seemingly unaware of the tension around him. Cecily stroked his fur while she read from her chapter book. Of course, the book had a black horse on the cover.

They had to dodge a few infected and take the long way around the city, as one of the roads had been blocked with abandoned cars. After driving for more than two hours, they were almost to Ashland's safe zone. They passed a burned out Walmart and several mobile home parks that looked like a bomb had gone off in the middle of it, before they turned onto the road leading to the school. It felt strange to go back there after everything that had happened.

"Pull to the front," John instructed Dan as the high school came into view.

"What's that?" Cecily asked, pointing to the sky. Thick, black smoke billowed from the back of the building.

Dan stomped on the brakes, and James almost slid off his seat, his seatbelt pulling tight across his chest.

"Sorry, sorry," Dan said, his hands tight on the steering wheel.

Four zombies lumbered toward the smoke but had turned around when the vehicle approached. They stumbled towards the van. More zombies lay dead on the road. John looked at Toby and nodded. The unspoken message was clear. They would kill the zombies.

"Are you ready?" John asked, pulling his shotgun from beneath the seat. Toby nodded, readying his own gun, and they jumped out of the van.

The air smelled of acrid smoke. It billowed from the other side of the building in puffy, black clouds. Cecily's book slipped out of her hand, landing with a thud on the floor beside her feet.

"Fire," Mom whispered, gripping the seat in front of her as she peered through the windshield. "Dan, the school is on fire."

John and Toby quickly took care of the infected before they could come any closer. Dan motioned for them to get back into the van then clicked on the radio.

"Stay inside your vehicles and hold your position." Dan spoke into the radio to the other vans pulling up behind them. "I'm going around back. Radio me if the fire attracts more of the infected. We don't want to get trapped back there."

Dan eased onto the dead grass, now thick with weeds, and drove towards the black smoke. After turning the corner of the building, Dan stopped the van, jumped out, and ran.

Chen, Parker, and Dotty were franticly trying to put out the fire. Chen had a garden hose pointed at the charred wall, but a pitiful amount of water trickled from it. The fire had spread to the attic and roof in vivid, red-orange streaks, the heat so intense, Dan staggered back. The black smoke spread across the sky. Parker threw buckets of water on the fire. It didn't seem to make any difference to the growing flames.

If there had been firefighters and trucks filled with water in the city, the school might have had a chance. As things were now, there was no way to save the school. The fire leapt, the bright flames spreading quickly in just the few seconds since they had arrived.

When Chen saw Dan running towards him, he dropped the hose and sank to the ground in defeat. James slipped out of the van and stepped closer. He wanted to hear what Chen was saying.

"We were attacked early this morning," Chen said to Dan. "A large group of infected smashed the glass doors and made it into the building. Most of the residents got out but not everyone, I'm sad to say. The survivors fled in the few vehicles we had left. During the fight, someone used a flare gun to try to kill the zombies. They missed and hit the school. By the time we realized what had happened, the fire was out of control." Chen swiped at the beads of sweat dripping down his face, leaving a streak of black soot.

"I'm so sorry. It's bad in Richmond too," Dan said, shaking his head. "We were overrun by a large horde of infected at the CDC. Admiral Walker asked me to come by and check on you before we left the state. We're heading to Cobb Island, Maryland.

You're welcome to join us. Are there more survivors?"
He looked from Chen to Dottie.

Dottie shook her head, her gray hair flying wildly around her, eyes red from the smoke. "It's just the three of us left now. Most of the residents fled in the few vehicles we had. We were the only ones who stayed to try to save the safe zone." She choked back tears. "If you have room, we'd better take you up on your offer. Ashland has become too dangerous, and now that we've lost the high school, there's no reason to stay."

Parker coughed, his hands on his knees, sucking in air. His hair was wet with sweat, his clothes dirty, and his face white. James didn't really want Parker to come with them, but they had nowhere else to go. Safety was the most important thing right now.

There was a loud boom as the storage shed, about twenty-five feet from where they were standing, exploded in a ball of flames. Everyone ducked for cover. When the smoke cleared a bit, the fire was roaring out of control. Dan motioned for everyone to stand back from the burning building and to take refuge behind the van.

"That storage shed contained the last of the gas we'd saved for the generator," Chen said, shaking his head.

The radio crackled.

"Dan here," he answered.

"Yeah, Dan this is Derrick. More infected have

noticed the fire and are coming this way. Are we ready to hit the road again? Victoria is getting pretty nervous." Baby Rose cried in the background.

"Yes, we'll be right there," Dan said.

Everyone piled in the van. It was tight quarters with three extra people, but nobody complained. One thing James had noticed—if times were tough, people pulled together to help those in need. It was reassuring, even if it did make for an uncomfortable ride.

[9]

AIDEN WALKED beside his father as they approached the big house. The President must have decided Aiden wasn't dangerous. He had invited Aiden and his dad to a formal dinner. Aiden hoped Ava would be allowed to attend. She had a way of making every-thing seem like a party. Besides, he didn't want to be the only kid there.

The tests looked promising, although no cure had been found yet. Dad thought they were getting close though. Aiden hoped that was true. Cobb Island was a nice place, but he missed being a regular kid. He missed his mom and his friends. He wished for his old life back but knew it would never be the same.

Two soldiers stood on the porch. They had rifles slung across their shoulders but seemed relaxed and nodded to Aiden as he climbed the steps to the entrance. Ava must have been waiting for him because as soon as they stepped on the porch she flung open the front door.

"Hi, Aiden. I'm glad you could come tonight. We're having dinner in the formal dining room, and then Daddy says we can play cards while the scientists talk. Do you like crazy eights, go fish, or war? I think we better play war because of your hands," Ava said in a rush as she pulled him inside the house. Coco danced around his ankles, tail wagging furiously.

It was strange to think that when Aiden had first arrived, they had wanted to strap him down to his cot and now he was invited to dine with the President of the United States. Okay, he couldn't really eat anything yet, but he *had* been able to drink juice and the scientists had put all kind of medicine and stuff in it to keep him alive. It tasted awful, but he didn't mind as long as he got better.

Ava led him to a large dining room at the back of the house. An oval mahogany table, gleaming with white-and-gold dishes, sat in the middle. A huge, sparkling crystal chandelier twinkled overhead, bouncing prisms of color across the ceiling.

It still seemed strange to be enjoying electricity when most of the world went without. Ava pulled out a chair for him, and he awkwardly sat down. Coco lay at Ava's feet, waiting for a scrap of food.

"The cooks made you your own soup, Aiden. Chicken and vegetables or something like that." She leaned closer and whispered, "Daddy says I can't eat any of your soup because it has special ingredients in it for your condition."

He wished he could ask her all the questions swirling around in his head, but he could only shrug and nod.

President Harrison and Admiral Walker entered the room along with Dr. Basheer, Dr. Takahashi, and Dr. Benton. They sat at the other end of the long table. Dad sat in the chair beside Dr. Benton. That was good. He could spill without embarrassing his dad.

"I heard you're making progress. That's amazing. I want to document every step of your recovery," Ava said and grabbed a roll from a basket, taking a big bite.

A bowl of thick, green soup was placed in front of him. How was he supposed to eat this? He'd probably spill it all over the fancy, white tablecloth.

He clumsily picked up his spoon and dipped it into the bowl. He brought the spoon to his mouth with an unsteady hand and tentatively took a taste. It wasn't too bad. It tasted like peas and carrots mixed with vitamins. He was secretly pleased to be able to sit and eat like a normal person. Ava ate her creamy potato soup with enjoyment. She didn't have to worry about spilling all over herself.

Ava was a nice girl and all that, but she was sheltered here on the island, surrounded by the best security available. She had no idea what it was really like out there. Aiden did. He'd wandered the streets by himself for days, wondering what was going to happen to him. He remembered how his mother had looked as she stumbled past him on the freeway. She was dead now, and there was no bringing her back.

[10]

JAMES AWOKE with a jolt as the van swerved around something in the road. It was dark outside, and they were traveling on some unknown road toward Maryland. It must have been several hours since they'd left Richmond, but it was slow going. He couldn't believe he'd actually fallen asleep. Maybe the craziness of the last few hours had finally caught up with him. Dan and John talked quietly in the front seat. Cecily was asleep with Cupcake cuddled on her lap.

A faint sniffling came from behind him, and he glanced around. Parker leaned against the window, and even though it was dark in the van, James saw a tear run down his face. Parker swiped at his cheek and pulled his baseball cap lower on his head. The poor kid had lost both his mom and his dad. He was an orphan now. That would be hard. At least James had his mom and sister.

The van slowed and turned onto a dirt road. James peered through the window. He was about to ask where they were going when Dan whispered to Mom, "John and I are beat. It's not safe to travel at night anyway, so we're going to stop here and rest for few hours. We'll get back on the road at first light."

Mom nodded and sat up straight in her seat, rubbing her neck

Cecily yawned and stretched. Ella whimpered but didn't wake up. The clock on the dashboard glowed red. It was 12:38.

They followed the road past several large oak trees before pulling in front of an old farmhouse. The wide porch that wrapped around the front was empty, the windows dark. James doubted anyone lived there now. He didn't think a *living* person was inside, anyway. He didn't know if they would find zombies. He hoped not. He was too tired to deal with all that. Besides, zombies smelled horrible.

The other vans pulled up behind them. Dan climbed out and walked quickly to the front door, rifle in hand. He flipped on a flashlight and slipped inside the dark house. James held his breath as he waited for Dan to give the all-clear signal. When Dan finally stepped back onto the porch and waved, James sighed with relief. Everyone stumbled from the vans, stretching and talking softly.

The house was dark inside, so John had gone in first to light a few lanterns. The room James entered was neat and tidy, as if waiting for the owners to return. The flickering lights spread shadows dancing across the walls, like the set of a horror movie. James shook his head. They were already living a nightmare.

"Where should I sleep?" James asked Mom when she entered the house with Cecily and Ella.

"There are three bedrooms upstairs," Dan said, gesturing to the staircase by the front door. "Why don't you guys take one, and the other families can have the other two?"

"I'll be fine on the sofa," John said. "I want to keep watch anyway."

Parker entered the room and brushed passed James, stomping through the house and out the back door. The screen door slammed loudly behind him. He stalked to a tree in the back and flopped down on the ground, his back against the trunk.

Dottie crossed the room to stand beside him. "Parker's having a rough time of it," she said softly, her voice full of concern.

James could only nod. He didn't know what to say. Everyone was having a rough time these days. Was it only a few weeks ago that he and Parker were doing skateboard tricks in Ashland's school gym? Neither one of them had a skateboard now, and it didn't seem to matter anymore. Survival had become the most important thing.

James followed his family up the stairs. The room was small with a queen-sized bed taking up most of the space. No way was there room for four people in that bed. Besides, this bedroom used to belong to a teenage girl,; complete with purple bedding and posters of boy bands. The dresser was strewn with makeup and earrings. Cecily sighed as she fingered a glittering bangle bracelet.

"I'll sleep on the floor," James offered.

Mom and the girls were tired, but he wasn't really sleepy. Mom helped Ella climb into the bed, and Cecily lay down beside her. James grabbed a pillow and blanket and lay on the floor. The full moon shone through the window. Soon everyone had settled down for the night.

It was hot in the house, and he tossed and turned on the hard floor. He kept remembering Parker's face as he wiped away his tears. He finally gave up and tiptoed to the window. There was a clear view of the backyard. The woods beyond the house loomed thick with trees, an empty field next to it where crops should have been planted ready for harvest. An old barn, its red paint chipped and peeling, stood beyond the tree Parker was under. He was probably asleep. James was about to return to his bed when he noticed movement in the trees beyond the tree.

What if there were zombies in the woods heading for Parker? What should he do? Maybe he should go tell Dan and John.

James quietly slipped from the room, as not to wake the others. He crept down the stairs. John was stretched out on the sofa, sound asleep. Dan was in a rocking chair, his head back, snoring softly. James didn't want to wake them up, but what if there were zombies in the woods?

The movement could have just been the breeze though. Maybe he should check it out, before waking everyone up.

He stepped carefully across the creaking wooden floorboards to the back door and slipped outside. The fresh air felt good on his warm cheeks. His eyes slowly scanned the area, but he saw nothing unusual. He tiptoed across the dead grass to where Parker lay.

"Hey, dude, wake up," he whispered, nudging him with his foot.

Parker rolled onto his back. When he realized he'd been asleep, Parker sat up quickly and rubbed his eyes. "What do *you* want, Hadley?" he muttered.

"I thought I saw something in the trees behind you. Maybe you should come into the house."

Parker's head whipped toward the tree line. Nothing was there. Not even a breeze stirred the branches. He glanced back at James with narrowed eyes. "Why? I'm not scared. Are you?" he challenged.

"No. I'm not sca—" he began but then stopped himself. Why not tell the truth? "Yes, actually, I *am* scared. I don't want to see anyone else get hurt."

Parker stared at James a moment longer then shrugged, leaning back against the tree. James was about to give up and return to the house when the trees rustled again. He turned to look just as a zombie burst through the trees. It was a woman with dark, stringy hair and a torn blue dress. She was followed by two men, and they staggered towards them.

"The infected are here, we've got to go!" James said.

Parker jumped up, but he tripped on a tree root, sprawling hard on the ground. The zombies advanced and were between them and the house. James looked around for a safe place to run. The only thing he could see was the barn. Maybe they could make it there and bar the door.

"The barn," he cried, and Parker staggered to his feet as the zombies closed in. They ran to the barn, but Parker was limping. He must have twisted his ankle when he fell.

The door was heavy and scraped on the uneven ground as James pulled it open. They slipped inside, but he couldn't pull the door shut behind him. It was stuck. They crossed to the middle of the dark barn, looking around frantically. The zombies were right behind them. James could make out several empty animal stalls, their gates broken and useless. There was nowhere to hide in there.

He spied a ladder leading up to a hay loft and helped Parker hobble over. Parker scrambled up as fast as his injured ankle would allow. James followed behind him. He had just reached the top when a zombie hit the ladder, sending it crashing to the ground. James slipped, his body dangling off the edge. Parker grabbed his arms and pulled. James swung his leg to the side and managed to pull himself onto the loft. The infected growled in frustration as they stared at James and Parker, just out of reach.

The boys sat in shock, the zombies circling around beneath them, like a pack of hungry wolves. James had thought their group was safe in the farmhouse, but seeing the zombies below reminded him they were not really safe. None of them were.

"Now what are we going to do? We're stuck in here," Parker whispered, his voice cracking with fear.

"We'll have to wait until morning when the others wake up. Dan will come looking for us," James replied.

Parker groaned and fell back onto the hay. James sat beside him. How did he always get into these situations? At least he had been able to warn Parker. He hoped whoever looked for them would be armed. He didn't want to think what would happen if Ella or Cecily came into the barn alone.

"You should have just let the zombies get me," Parker muttered beside him, rubbing his rapidly swelling ankle.

James glanced at Parker in surprise. He never thought Parker, or anyone else for that matter, would actually want to die. Maybe losing his parents *had* really gotten to Parker, like he had suspected.

"I'm sorry about your mom and dad," James said, softly.

He felt bad for Parker and didn't know what else to say. He wished he could somehow go back in time and stop the stupid virus, but he couldn't. Mom said all they could do was survive one day at a time.

"Yeah, me too," Parker whispered, so softly James almost didn't hear him.

James sighed and lay down in the hay beside Parker. He stared into the darkness. Parker's sadness floated heavily in the air, mingling with the moans of the zombies. James would try to be nicer to Parker from now on.

[11]

AIDEN MANAGED to eat half the soup and was relieved that he only spilled a few drops on his shirt. It felt like progress, even if it was a small thing. But he knew he was the main topic of discussion. He was uncomfortably aware of the scientists at the other end of the table glancing at him throughout the meal.

"Let's go to my room," Ava said as soon as they finished eating. "If you don't want to play cards, I have Monopoly, Parcheesi, or Checkers. I also have some video games."

Aiden shrugged and nodded. He didn't think he could hold on to playing cards and doubted he could use a video game controller either.

As they walked around the table toward the stairs, everyone stopped talking, and all eyes turned to him. He shifted nervously from one foot to the other.

"Is everything all right, Aiden?" Dad asked.

Aiden nodded uncomfortably as all eyes turned to him.

"I'll come get you in a few minutes," Dad said.

Ava and Aiden made their escape out of the dining room. She pointed to the curved staircase.

"My room's up there. Come on," she said and, picking up Coco, started up the stairs. Aiden followed at a slower pace, holding tight to the railing and taking one stair at a time. It really sucked being a zombie.

Once he reached the top of the stairs, they walked down a long hallway until they stopped by a door at the end. Ava's room was what he had expected for the President's daughter. It had a dark wood canopy bed with gauzy, white fabric tied back from the posts. It was covered in a pink-and-purple floral bedspread, with a large stuffed kitty and a lamb perched next to an abundance of pillows. A small, round table and two chairs sat beneath a picture of the ocean at sunset, the perfect spot to play games. A stack of comic books were strewn across the table. It all seem so normal, which was strange considering the craziness of the rest of the country.

"How about this one?" Ava asked, pulling the Monopoly box from a bookcase next to the window.

Aiden shrugged and watched as she cleared the comics off the table and began setting up the game. He walked slowly around the room, the plush carpet soft beneath his sneakers. This was the perfect room for a girl. Cecily would have loved it. He remembered the kids would be arriving soon, and that cheered him up. His heart raced in excitement just thinking about his friends.

He tried to play the game, he really did, but he dropped the pieces easily and Ava had to take over for him. They played for about thirty minutes before she became frustrated and gave up completely. He didn't blame her. She snapped a picture of him sitting at the table before putting the game away.

"Now what should we do?" Ava said, looking around the room.

Aiden didn't want to stay up here. It was warm upstairs and he couldn't really play the games anyway.

"Out..." he managed to mumble, and Ava clapped in delight.

"Did you say *out*? Oh my gosh, Aiden, that's amazing!" she cried. "Do you want to go outside?"

He nodded in relief. She had understood what he was trying to say.

They left the bedroom and slowly made their way back downstairs.

"This way. There's a back door. We don't want to disturb anyone," Ava said, wrinkling her nose and motioning to the dining room. Aiden glanced through the open door. It looked like everyone had finished eating and was having coffee and talking.

They tiptoed quietly down the hall toward the

back of the house. Aiden passed a closed door when he heard his name. He stopped and turned to listen. It was amazing how clearly he could hear their voices, even with the door closed. He pressed his ear against the cool wood. Ava stepped next to him and did the same thing, her head next to his on the door.

"We have no choice, Dr. Benton. This work is of the utmost important for the survival of mankind. I don't like it any more than you do, but if we don't take advantage of the opportunity to study *all* of Aiden's anatomy, we could miss something vital. You know I'm right."

There was silence for a moment. Aiden glanced at Ava. Her eyes were huge in her round face.

"Dr. Winter's will never agree to an autopsy. Aiden's his only son."

"Then we'll proceed without his consent. Once it's done, it'll be too late to stop it."

What were they planning to do to him? Wasn't an autopsy when they cut up a dead body to see what had happened to the person? Did they want to do that to him?

Ava gasped, covered her mouth with her hand, and pulled him down the hall. She peeked around the door and, seeing no one, pulled him outside and onto the back porch. Coco barked softly.

"Quiet, Coco," Ava whispered, picking up the dog then turned to face Aiden. "We won't let them do that to you. We have to find a place for you to hide."

She paced up and down the porch for a moment thinking.

Aiden's stomach knotted in fear. The scientists meant to kill him so they could study his body. How could he stop them? He was just a kid.

Ava stopped walking and turned to him excitedly. "I've got it. I found some maps of the island in my room. There are some caves on the other side of the island. We can hide in there for a few days. At least until we figure out what to do. We need more time. You're getting better every day. Even I can see that. Those stupid scientists can't be allowed to hurt you."

Aiden shrugged. He wished he could talk to his dad and tell him everything he had heard. But it sounded like the scientists didn't care if his dad agreed or not. His best option, for right now, was to do what Ava suggested and hide somewhere.

Ava peered into the darkness. "I think it would be better to follow the beach to the other side of the island. We should stay off the main road."

Footsteps sounded along the porch followed by deep voices. The soldiers were coming their way. Ava grabbed Aiden's hand and pulled him down the step onto the wide lawn. They ran as quickly as he could manage until they were under the cover of the trees.

"Give me a few minutes to grab some supplies, and I'll come back and get you," Ava said.

Aiden stared at her, eyes wide. What if she didn't return? Maybe she wouldn't be allowed back outside.

She sensed his worry and hugged him quickly. "It'll be okay. If I don't come back in ten minutes, follow the beach to where the land curves. There is a hotel there called The Whaler's Inn. Hide in the trees next to it. I'll find a way to meet you there."

He nodded, swallowing the lump in his throat. He'd thought he was finally safe when he found his dad and they'd come to the island. He was wrong. Ava's eyes sparkled like this was all a great big adventure and ran back to the house. It was more than an adventure, though. It was his life.

Aiden waited as a long as he dared. After about ten minutes, he started to panic. Should he wait longer? He shuffled back and forth beneath the trees. Another few minutes passed, and he couldn't wait any longer. He walked along the tree line until he reached the shore. It was slow going as his sneakers filled with sand. He stumbled along for about twenty minutes before dropping onto a piece of driftwood to rest.

It was dark. With no street lights or electricity on the island, he wouldn't have been able to see enough to even walk on the beach. Luckily, the moon reflected off the water as the waves gently lapped along the shore.

Was Ava coming or had she been stopped by the soldiers?

Breathing deeply, he wondered how far it was to the Whaler's Inn. He'd better keep going before someone noticed he was gone and came looking.

He had just set off down the beach again when something moved in the grass along the shore line. He stepped closer. A girl about his age, slowly stood up. She was dressed in jeans and a black T-shirt. Her dark hair was secured loosely in a ponytail.

"Hi, I'm Katie," she said, stepping forward, "and I know who you are. You're Aiden, right?"

Aiden nodded, surprised. Who was this girl, and how did she know who he was? Where did she come from? Wasn't she afraid of him? He thought the island had been cleared of people except the military.

"You're the zombie boy the government hopes will cure the virus."

He nodded again. How did she know?

"I can see I'd better explain a few things," she said, moving closer. "I've been watching everything that's been going on at the big house. That's *my* house, by the way," she said in a huff. "My parents were in Europe on business, and I was left with my nanny, Mary. After the virus broke out, Mary got scared or something because she said she was going out for an hour but never came back."

Katie smiled slightly and waved a hand.

"It's okay," she said. "I'm almost thirteen. It's not like I'm a baby or anything. I'm sure my parents will come back for me as soon as they can. When the President and his staff arrived, I hid. I didn't want them to send me off the island to some safe zone somewhere like they had done to everyone else. My parents might never find me if that happened." Katie glanced around nervously. "What are you doing out here alone?"

Aiden swallowed back his frustration. He wished he could ask her all the questions running through his head. Like, where has she been hiding, and how she had survived this long by herself?

Just then Ava came into view, running down the beach, Coco in her arms. She had a backpack thrown over her shoulder and a blanket around her neck. When she reached them, she leaned on her knees to catch her breath. Her eyes almost bulged out of her head when she spotted Katie.

"Who are you?" Ava gasped.

"I'm Katie. And you're Ava. You're sleeping in my bedroom," Katie said with a smirk.

Ava gaped, shifting from one foot to the other. "Really? That's cool. I mean, I'm sorry and all, but it's great there's another girl on the island." Ava glanced behind her and said, "We have to go, Aiden. The soldiers are searching the island for us."

"You'd better come with me. I have a place you can hide tonight. You can tell me what's going on later," Katie said.

"We were planning to hide in a cave on the other side of the island," Ava replied.

"I've lived on this island since I was five years old. I know every cave and beach around here. Most caves fill with water at high tide. You shouldn't hide in there."

"Aiden, where are you, Aiden?" a voice called from somewhere down the beach. They had to move quickly.

"Ava, are you out here?" a different voice said. They sounded closer now.

"Let's go," Ava whispered.

They followed Katie through the sand for another mile until they veered off the beach and into a grove of trees. Crossing the street, they passed underneath a house that was raised on pilings to prevent flooding during ocean storms. They walked past several cars and entered a backyard.

A large treehouse took up a corner of the yard. It was raised at least ten feet in the air and could only be accessed by climbing the wooden slats nailed into the trunk. It would make a pretty sweet fort or clubhouse, Aiden thought, but in this situation, he wasn't so sure about hiding up there. He didn't even know if he'd be able to climb up it.

Katie quickly scrambled up the wooden rungs and opened the small door.

"Come on, Aiden," Ava said, climbing up a few steps. She handed the dog up to Katie. Coco whimpered and barked. "Shhh, quiet," Ava commanded.

With some effort and a lot of pulling from Katie and Ava, Aiden made it up and into the treehouse. Several blankets were spread across the floor. More blankets were piled in the corner. Boxes of crackers, cookies, and soda were stacked in the other corner.

Katie switched on a flashlight, covering the bulb with her hand to dim the light. "This was my friend, Mark's, house. His family left for the safe zone with everyone else. They had a lot of supplies in their house though. Sometimes I'd sneak back into my own house and take things from the pantry, but that became harder once you arrived, Aiden. There's more soldiers patrolling the house now."

"Aiden, Ava!" Someone call nearby.

Everyone froze. Katie switched off the flashlight. Ava clamped a hand over Coco's muzzle to prevent her from barking. Heavy footsteps crunched the ground as several soldiers passed by. Aiden didn't think they entered the backyard, or they probably would have looked inside the treehouse.

Silence settled over them once more as they waited to make sure the soldiers had moved on. After a few tense minutes Katie crossed her arms and looking questioningly at Ava. Katie said, "Okay, do you want to tell me what you're running away from? Why are you hiding Aiden?"

"We were at dinner tonight and overheard the scientists talking about killing Aiden so they could study his body," Ava said, her eyes fierce. "We had to hide him. They said they were going to do it whether Dr. Winters, Aiden's dad, agreed or not."

"That's just dumb. I mean, Aiden's a walking

miracle." Katie shook her head. "We need to come up with a plan. We can't go anywhere in the dark, though. Especially with the soldiers looking for you. Hiding won't be any easier tomorrow either." She pointed at Ava and Aiden. "You're the President's daughter, and you're the hope for the cure. *Everyone* will be looking for you two. We'll have to be extra careful."

Katie yawned widely and shook her head. She lay down on the makeshift bed.

Aiden sighed. He didn't want his dad to worry about him, but it couldn't be helped. Still, he didn't think this wasn't a very good hideout. With his limited abilities, he couldn't climb down quickly. He hoped they found somewhere better tomorrow.

Ava yawned too and lay down on the blanket next to Katie. He sighed, laying down on the blanket next to Ava. He closed his eyes and, in a moment, drifted off to sleep.

[12]

THE PALE, golden rays of sunrise crept through the slats of the barn as dawn approached. James couldn't sleep anyway, and he was glad the night was over. The moans of the undead never stopped. Plus, worry about what would happen when they were discovered missing swirled around his brain until he thought he would go crazy.

Parker had fallen asleep after an hour, although he'd tossed and turned, moaning along with the zombies. His ankle looked sore and swollen.

The screen door to the house slammed shut, and James sat up.

"James, Parker!" his mom yelled, her voice frantic.

"We're in the barn, up in the loft," James yelled back. "There are zombies in here, Mom. Be careful!"

Parker sat up quickly and grabbed his throbbing

ankle. He glanced around wildly, his eyes red and puffy. More voices joined Mom's. The zombies stumbled out of the barn attracted to the noise. A moment later, the pop of gunfire exploded as the men took care of the undead.

James sighed in relief as his mom entered the barn, Dan beside her.

"James Hadley, what are you doing up there?" Mom asked, hands on hips.

"Get us down, and I'll tell you everything," James said.

Parker glanced at him and then looked away quickly. He probably thought James was going to blame him for everything.

Dan grabbed the ladder the zombies had knocked over and climbed up.

"I sprained my ankle," Parker said. "I don't think I can walk on it." He pulled up his pants leg to reveal his ankle, swollen to twice its normal size.

"Patty, will you see if you can locate something to bandage Parker's ankle?" Dan asked.

Mom nodded and, with a shake of her head, left the barn.

Dan glanced at Parker. "Once we get your ankle supported, you should be able to put enough weight on your leg to climb down the ladder."

"Okay, I'll try," Parker mumbled.

Dan climbed up the last few rungs and sat beside

the in the hay. Glancing from James to Parker, he asked, "Do you boys want to tell me how you ended up here?"

"It was hot in the bedroom upstairs, and I couldn't sleep," James began. "I thought I'd go talk to Parker and get some fresh air. We were just hanging out and talking and were about to go back inside when the zombies came out of the woods. They blocked the house so we ran to the barn. Parker tripped and hurt his ankle. We climbed up here and decided to wait it out."

Dan nodded slowly. James decided to skip the part where he'd asked Parker to come inside, and he'd refused. It wouldn't change anything, and Parker had enough to deal with already.

"I'm glad you boys are okay, but next time, stay inside where we know you're safe. You could have been killed today." Dan's voice was low and serious.

Parker looked like he wanted to cry. James swallowed the lump in his throat and nodded.

Mom burst into the barn, followed by Dottie and Wilma.

After Dan carefully bandaged Parker's ankle, they made their way down the ladder. Mom helped Parker hobble back to the house. James was surprised that Parker didn't moan and carry on and make a huge deal about his ankle. Maybe they had both grown up a little the past month.

Once inside the farmhouse, Mom sat Parker on a chair, and Wilma examined his ankle.

"I wish we had an ice pack to reduce the swelling," Wilma said, frowning. "You'd best keep that leg elevated, Parker,"

"We need to keep moving everyone. Captain Reynolds will be waiting for us," John said.

"Thanks for your help with the boys, Wilma," Dan said. "We'll load up and get on the road as soon as we can."

Mom passed out granola bars for breakfast, and everyone piled into the vans. James was extra squished in the seat because of Parker's leg, but they made it work.

"I never heard you leave the room last night," Cecily whispered. She shot him an accusing look.

"I didn't want to wake you," he said, shrugging.

"Don't go anywhere without me again. We have to stick together," she demanded,

hands on her hips. She looked angry, but her lips trembled. She was scared too. James was glad Cecily missed out on that particular bit of excitement.

The group made pretty good time once they got back on the main road. They passed a few abandoned cars and had to swerve around debris that littered the streets. James had just begun to relax when they came around a bend in the road and Dan suddenly slammed on the brakes. The other vans braked behind them.

A large group of zombies filled the road. Maybe fifty or more.

Dan grabbed the radio as bodies slammed into the van. "Move steadily forward. Try not to damage your vehicle. Remain calm and press forward and we should make it out."

He sounded calm, but James thought he was trying not to scare anyone more than they already were. The face of a man pressed against the window next to James. The zombie hissed and moaned, clawing at the glass as he tried to reach James. Ella screamed. Mom pulled her close to comfort her, but Mom looked terrified too.

Hands beat steadily on the side of the vehicles, battering the metal and leaving black smudges on the paint. It was gross and frightening at the same time. They drove steadily forward. Eventually, they made it through the horde of infected and picked up speed.

James looked back at the zombies stumbling after them. He breathed a sigh of relief and watched the road. No more infected were in the road that he could see.

They had just reached a sign that read, "Mathews:12 miles" when the van began to wobble and slow.

"I think we have a flat tire," Dan said as they pulled to a stop in the road.

Dang. James was beginning to wonder if they'd ever make it to the boat.

"Oh no, and we're so close," Mom said.

"Don't worry. We have a spare. We'll have the tire changed in a few minutes." Dan said.

Everyone climbed out of the van except Parker. He stayed in his seat with his leg elevated, looking sullenly out of the window. John and Toby stood guard, their guns at the ready, as Dan jacked up the vehicle.

"I need to go to the bathroom," Ella said, glancing up at Mom with round, scared eyes. After the horde of zombies they'd encountered a few minutes ago, he didn't blame her for being afraid.

"I'll take you to the ladies' bush," Mom joked. "Anyone else care to join us?"

"I'll go," Cecily said, handing Cupcake to James.

He walked to the edge of the road and set the kitten down in the grass. Maybe it needed a potty break too. Cupcake immediately scampered away, and James had to chase after it. Once he finally caught the kitten, he sat in the overgrown grass, stroking it's soft fur and wondering what would have happened to it if Cecily hadn't come along when she did.

Dan had just finished changing the tire when Mom, Ella, and Cecily returned. Everyone climbed back into the vans. James handed Cupcake to Cecily.

The wind whipped the trees, and the sky was turning dark. A thunderstorm was moving into the area. They had no shelter other than the vans and very little food. He crossed his fingers and prayed the boat was waiting for them when they finally made it to the dock. If it wasn't, he didn't know what they'd do.

13

Dr. Benton leaned over Aiden, a large needle in his gloved hand. The other scientists stood beside Aiden, holding his arms as he struggled to get away. He glanced around wildly. His dad stood just inside the doorway. He tried to call to him, but nothing came out of his mouth except a terrified moan.

"I'm sorry, Aiden, but we have to do this. It's for science and the future of mankind," Dad said before turning away. The needle plunged into Aiden's arm just as he screamed, "No!"

"Aiden. Wake up, Aiden," Katie said. "You're having a bad dream."

He sat up quickly, sweat dripping down his back. His heart beat double time as he tried to catch his breath. He was in the treehouse with Ava and Katie. He let out a long breath. Coco snuggled up next to him, licking his hand, trying to comfort him in his doggy way.

"You were yelling, Aiden, but you spoke clearly. You should try to talk more. I think it's a sign that you're getting better," Ava said, excitedly.

Katie crawled over to the door and cracked it open. She peered outside for a minute, the bright sunlight streaming in the room, before closing the door and coming back inside. "We better find a different location to hide. There are lots of homes and business on the island that are abandoned. I'm sure we can find somewhere that they'll never look," Katie said, turning to Ava. "What's your plan?"

"My what?" Ava asked.

"Well, you can't hide forever. What will you do to convince the scientists that they should spare Aiden?"

"I haven't thought that far." Ava frowned, twirling a piece of hair between her fingers. "When my dad finds out I'm missing, he'll be really worried. If we wait a day or two before going back, he'll be so happy to see me that he'll agree to save Aiden." She smiled slyly. "He's the President, so the scientists have to do what he says."

"I guess." Katie shrugged, glancing at Aiden.

He shifted uncomfortably. He hated that he couldn't talk. It made him feel useless. He had some ideas and wanted to contribute to their plans.

"Ho...tel," he stuttered, the sound feeling odd as it escaped his lips.

The girls jumped and turned to look at him, their eyes wide. Maybe they had forgotten he was even there.

"Hi...de, ho...tel," he said again, pleased that they could understand what he was trying to say.

"Good idea, Aiden. There are lots of rooms in the hotel, and I'm sure we could find a key somewhere," Ava said, nodding. "Let go to the Whaler's Inn I told you about."

Aiden nodded, relieved that she had understood him..

Ava turned to Katie. "Do you know where that is?"

"Of course. It's a few miles down the road, but I think the soldiers will check the rooms there." Katie crossed her arms, thinking for a moment. "I know a better place. Let's go to the old lighthouse. It's a bit farther away, but I think it has the perfect hiding spot. The challenge will be getting there without being caught."

"Okay, you know the town better than I do. Let's go," Ava said, gathering up her backpack.

Suddenly there was movement below them, and they froze in place.

"I'm going to check up there," a deep voice said gruffly.

Aiden tensed in anticipation. The soldiers had returned. Were they about to be discovered? Ava grabbed Coco, and they scooted to the corner of the treehouse. But there was no place to hide in the small space.

"Never mind that, Sargent Green," another man said. "We're needed on the other side of the island. This area has already been searched anyway."

The voices of the soldiers faded as they walked away. Aiden peeked through the wooden slats of the treehouse as the soldiers disappeared around the front of the house. He sighed in relief. They were safe for now, but they had to be careful. Everyone was looking for them.

"Whew, that was close. We should cut through the backyards and alleys behind the houses. I've gotten pretty good at hiding the last few weeks, so follow me," Katie whispered proudly.

Aiden and Ava nodded. One at a time, they carefully climbed down the tree. He hated that it took him longer than the girls. He was relieved when his feet touched the ground and he hadn't fallen on his butt. That would have been embarrassing.

They followed Katie through a hedge at the side of the house and into the next yard. The sun was quickly heating up the day, but the wind whistling through the trees kept them cool. Distant thunder made Aiden glance up. Dark clouds were building in the sky behind them, and it wouldn't be long until it began to rain. It would suck to get wet, but it was better than being captured by the scientists.

They trudged along, hiding behind buildings or

trees whenever they heard voices or a vehicle passed by. It was strange to see so much activity on the streets. The island had become a ghost town when the people were relocated to a safe zone, securing the area for the President and his team of scientists.

They had just rounded the corner of a white clapboard-sided building with a sign that read, "The Salty Sailor Seafood Shack," when two soldiers stepped from the entrance onto the street. They were followed by Admiral Walker. Aiden moved back, and the girls retreated behind him, peering around the corner.

"The President is furious, and heads will roll if those kids aren't found today," the Admiral said, frowning as a fat drop of rain hit his face.

The raindrops increased until the sky opened up, and it began to pour. The soldiers raced to a Jeep that was waiting across the street. The Admiral climbed in beside them. As they drove away, Aiden didn't mind in the least that he was getting soaked. The soldiers had gone.

The girls felt differently though. Ava squealed and pulled a little blanket out of her backpack, using it as an umbrella to cover herself, Coco, and Katie.

Aiden wanted to sit down on the wet pavement and cry. Instead, he raised his face to the dark blue sky and let the rain trickle down his checks. He was more afraid than he'd ever been since this whole awful virus began. Eventually, they would be discovered. They couldn't hide forever.

He shuddered and closed his eyes. What would happen to him then?

14

JAMES HELD his breath as the caravan of vehicles neared the town of Mathews. The storm had finally passed, and the sun peeked through the clouds. Dan dodged wrecked cars, garbage, and empty trash bags as he drove. James cringed when he saw a kid's shoe in the middle of the road. He wondered where the other shoe was. There was probably a one-shoed zombie kid wondering around somewhere.

They'd passed several deserted houses and a couple of infected, but the last few miles had been fairly quiet. When they drove along a stretch of ocean shoreline, he knew they were getting close. Relief coursed through him. Just a few more minutes and they would be there.

They rounded a bend in the road. Down a small hill was the boat ramp. A huge, gray boat with U.S. Coast Guard painted in bright orange letters across the side bobbed gently against the dock. Cecily cheered, and Mom smiled, wiping away a tear of happiness. They had made it in time. The boat was waiting for them.

All three vans parked alongside the dock. Dan and John climbed out of the van. Dan left his door open as he glanced around, rifle in his hand. Chen joined them and scrubbed his hands over his face as they surveyed the large vessel. It bobbed gently against the dock, but no one came out to greet them. It was eerily quiet.

"Everyone, wait inside your vehicle while we check out the boat and make sure it's safe," Dan said.

"Can I get out of the van? I'm sick of being cooped up in here," Parker complained.

"It'll be just another few minutes, okay? I don't see anyone around, and I was told we'd be met by the Coast Guard."

"Be careful, Dan," Mom said worriedly.

The men stood looking at the boat for several minutes. No one came out to greet them. The boat that had been waiting for them appeared to be deserted. Who knew what Dan would find once he got inside? Maybe it was full of the infected, or maybe the crew had abandoned the boat for some reason. Whatever had happened, it probably wouldn't be good news. James's heart beat quickened as he glanced around. It was quiet except for the chirping of a few birds. He hoped Dan, Chen, or one of the other men knew how to operate such a large boat.

Cecily scooted closer to him on the blue vinyl seat of the van. She slipped her hand into his as the men approached the dock warily. They each carried hand guns and had knives strapped to their waist and rifles across their backs. They were prepared for a fight. Dan climbed aboard the boat first, followed by John and Chen.

"Hey, anyone in there?" Dan called, banging his knife against the metal railing like a dinner bell. James hoped the men weren't going to be on the menu.

At first, nothing happened, and James thought maybe everything was going to be okay. But then a zombie stumbled onto the deck, heading for the men. He was a middle-aged man, dressed in a white navel officer's uniform, which was now streaked dark red with blood. His clawed hands reached out for Dan as he staggered towards the men.

Dan stepped back and fired at the zombie, who fell heavily at Dan's feet. The crack of the gunshot rang out in the quiet morning air, echoing around the dock, and soon more infected joined the party, pouring out of the front and back of the boat. James quickly counted ten zombies, all dressed in military uniforms. Toby and Jeff jumped from their vehicles to aid in the fight.

Ella whimpered in fear, and Mom pulled her onto her lap. He'd seen the infected killed before, but it was still an awful thing to watch. Two more infected appeared and more shots rang out. It seemed like forever, but was probably only a few minutes before the last zombie was down.

John motioned for everyone to stay in the vans while he, Dan, and Chen entered the boat. Toby and Jeff stood watch on the boat deck, scanning the area, guns out and ready.

"What happened to the all soldiers, Patty?" Ella whispered. She raised a frightened face to his mom.

"I'm afraid the boat was overrun with infected," Mom said, stroking Ella's dark hair. Mom swiped at another tear, but this time she wasn't crying from happiness.

James glanced at Parker, who was staring down at his hands, his face white. James swallowed past the lump in his throat. Parker's dad, Frank, had been killed by zombies. James wished he knew something to say that would make Parker feel better, but since he didn't, he stayed silent.

Everyone waited nervously for several tense minutes. Dan returned to the vans while Toby, Jeff, and the others cleared the deck of the zombies they had taken care of.

"We've searched the boat, and it's clear of any infected. Everyone bring your Bug Out Bags, and we'll board the ship. I'd like us to stay in the main areas. Let's keep everyone together. We've come this far, and I don't want to risk an accident." Dan seemed to be speaking to the parents, warning them to keep the kids close. Baby Rose cried from the other van, and James hoped the noise didn't attract more infected.

He sighed in relief when he was finally allowed to exit the van. He pulled his backpack onto his back and waited for Parker.

"I don't think anyone expected that." James said, turning to Parker.

"Nope," Parker mumbled, swinging his own pack onto his back. He glanced at James quickly then away. Kicking a pebble and shifting from one foot to the other, Parker said, "Uh, thanks for warning me about the zombies last night."

"Sure, I mean, that's what friends are for, right?" James said. He glanced at Parker and wondered what he would think about James being his *friend*.

Parker shrugged but seemed to walk a little taller as they followed the group up the ramp and onto the boat.

[15]

AIDEN TRIED to keep up with Ava and Katie as they moved quickly from house to house, but several times the girls had to wait for him to catch up. Poor Coco was practically dragged by Ava. The curious little dog would stop and investigate their surroundings, until Ava finally picked him up and carried him. Hiding was easy though. He'd played night games with his friends for years. The hide and seek game, Ghost in the Graveyard, had been one of his favorites. Only this time, it was more than a game, —it was life or death.

They hid behind fences or garbage cans when the soldiers passed by. He always knew when they were coming though. It was strange, but in the last day or so, some of his senses, like hearing and sight, seemed sharper, almost painfully so. He could hear the buzzing of the bees or even the flapping of the bird's wings as if they were right beside his ear. He could see things clearly, even things that were small and far away. He'd always had good eye sight, but now it was like bionic vision or something. He could read small print and see the fine details of trees and plants.

He hadn't said anything to the girls yet, afraid it was some temporary side effect from the vaccinations they had tested on him. It was kind of cool though. He hoped it was a positive side effect of the virus. It would be nice if something good happened, after all the bad things the world had endured.

A soft buzz overhead caused Aiden to stop walking. He listened carefully. Something was coming towards them. Grabbing Ava's arm, he pulled her to a stop.

Katie turned and looked at them. "What is it?" she asked softly.

Aiden pointed to the sky.

"Hide," he said, motioning for Ava and Katie to crawl under an old wooden picnic table next to them. Everyone scrambled underneath.

The buzzing grew really loud now. It circled around the house and hovered overhead. A military drone. They were using everything they could to find them. After several tense moments, the drone finally flew off.

Aiden sighed in relief. They were safe for now.

"It's not far to the lighthouse," Katie said. "It's just at the end of the next road."

"Coco's thirsty," Ava said. She pulled a bottle of water from her backpack and cupped her hand, making a little bowl for the dog to drink from. Most of the water seeped through her fingers, but the dog seemed happy to have the little drink.

They crawled from beneath the table and moved quickly through the overgrown grass. Aiden was hot and tired from running. He wanted to stop and rest, but he wouldn't feel safe until he was off the streets. There were fewer houses around as they got closer to the lighthouse, as they were at the farthest point of the island and away from the main part of town. Aiden glanced around as they ran from tree to tree. He could hear the surf as it broke against the shore. He loved the clean salty smell of the ocean, but he didn't like being exposed like they were, out in the open.

"The beach leading to the lighthouse is just down this path," Katie said, brushing the hair back from her sweaty brow.

The black roof of the lighthouse came into view, towering over the treetops. They walked carefully along the shore, the area covered in large rocks rather than sand. They stopped. The land dropped off into a steep cliff. The shore here was rocky and dangerous. He could see why a lighthouse was built on this spot.

Aiden glanced around, but they seemed to be totally alone. He breathed deeply of the fresh air, the ocean spray cooling his skin. The lighthouse was tall, at least sixty feet high. The body of the building was painted in white and black stripes. Attached at the bottom was a white cottage with black shutters and a red front door. A closed sign hung in the window.

"Before the virus outbreak, they offered guided tours here," Katie said. "This used to be a fort a long time ago but was converted into a home for the lighthouse keepers."

"How is this a good place to hide? It's cool and all that, but it seems like a place the soldiers would look for sure," Ava said.

"Follow me, and you'll see," Katie said. She wiggled the knob on the red door. "Locked," she said. "I figured. Come on. I have another idea."

She led them around the other side of the cottage to a row of bushes. She pushed one aside to reveal a small basement window. It was pretty narrow, but they were kids and small still. Maybe they could squeeze through it. Ava looked Aiden over.

"I think we'll all fit," she said, nodding. She rubbed Coco's head. He sniffed the air and whined.

Katie pulled on the window, but it barely moved an inch. Ava joined her and tugged harder. After a few minutes, they were able to slide the window open enough that they could wiggle through. Katie slid in first. Ava handed Coco to Katie and then followed her into the dark basement.

Aiden rocked from side to side. If the girls could climb down there, he was going to do it too. He had to, he reminded himself, as he slowly lowered himself into the dark basement. He slipped down behind Ava, almost falling as he hit the floor with a thud. It was dark and musty down here. Ava sneezed twice. Aiden took a few steps forward. He could almost feel the spiders crawling up his leg. He bit back a scream when something brushed against his face.

Squinting into the darkness, he saw it was just a string attached to a light bulb. It dangled overhead from a wooden beam. Katie pulled the string, but of course no light came on. There was no electricity here.

In the dim light, Aiden could just make out several shelves of mason jars. Rows and rows of peaches, pears, beets, and tomatoes were placed neatly in a line. There were small statues of the light-house, along with boxes of yoyos and playing cards. They had price tags on them. These were items sold in the gift shop. Perfect. If they had to hide down here, at least they wouldn't go hungry. There were boxes stacked along one wall. Probably more supplies for the store.

"I'm going upstairs to check it out. You guys stay here until I give you the all-clear," Katie said. She crossed the room, tiptoeing up the stairs before slowly turning the handle of the door that led to the cottage.

"It's creepy down here," Ava whispered, setting Coco on the old stone floor. The little beagle pranced around, sniffing the air.

He'd rather be down here. It wasn't as scary as being hunted by the soldiers.

Katie returned after a minute. "It's all clear up there. Plus, I found this."

She held up a bag of saltwater taffy in every color of the rainbow. She ripped open the bag and gave them each a piece. Aiden managed to pull off the wrapper and popped the treat into his mouth. The sweet taste of strawberries melted on his tongue. He wished he could enjoy the candy, but he couldn't help worry the soldiers were going to find them any minute.

Ava spread her blanket on the floor, and they stretched out in front of an old wood-burning stove that had been used to heat the building. Luckily, it was summer, and although it was cool in the basement, it wasn't really cold.

"They say this place is haunted," Katie said around a mouthful of taffy. "Hundreds of years ago, a ship wrecked here before the lighthouse was build. They say Old Captain Bart walks the cliffs and haunts the lighthouse, warning others of danger."

"Really? That is *so* cool. Do you think we'll see any ghosts?" Ava said, eagerly.

Katie shrugged. "Who knows?"

Aiden didn't really believe in ghosts, but he couldn't help the small shiver that ran down his spine. He glanced around the dark basement, but all he saw was dust and cobwebs.

He was suddenly tired. He hadn't really slept much last night. Lying down on the blanket, he closed his eyes and hoped James and Cecily would arrive on the island soon. He didn't know when he'd see them again though. They were on the run now, and he didn't know when it would be safe to return back to his dad.

Aiden was almost asleep when a loud thump sounded above them, followed by the sound of breaking glass. Heavy boots clomped across the floor overhead. The soldiers were in the cottage.

[16]

EVERYONE HUDDLED in the main area of the ship. Metal benches, painted gray like the boat, sat in neat rows, and everyone found a seat. The little boys, Liam and Jonah, jumped from bench to bench, climbing and playing until their dad, Derrick, pulled them onto his lap. Victoria held a sleeping baby Rose in her arms. The other families filled up the seats.

James, Cecily, and Parker sat by a window with Mom and Ella beside them. Dan, John, Chen, and the others disappeared into the bridge to figure out how to get the boat running.

James gazed around him. He hoped they'd cleared all the infected from the boat. They'd had enough setbacks already. Parker rubbed his ankle, propping it up on the bench in front of him. Dottie noticed his discomfort and, digging into her bug out bag, pulled out two aspirin, handing them to Parker with a bottle of water.

The engine roared to life. Everyone cheered, the mood suddenly lighter. James let out a long breath in relief. They were going to make it to the island.

Toby untied the thick ropes holding the boat to the dock and jumped aboard. They slowing pulled away from the shore, heading to open water. In a few hours, they would be at Cobb Island. James sighed in relief. He'd come to care about everyone in their little group, and it was a relief to think that soon they'd all be safe.

"I need to go to the bathroom," Parker muttered to Dottie.

"Oh, umm, let's see," she said, looking around. A sign said, "Toilets" with an arrow pointing down a set of stairs.

"I'll go with him," James said. He was too nervous to sit still. He wanted to move around anyway, so he might as well go with Parker. Besides, he'd promised himself that he would be nicer to him.

The boat picked up speed as they approached the open water. Parker held onto James as they made their way carefully down the stairs. Once at the bottom, there were several doors on either side of the hallway. One was marked restrooms, but he wondered what was in the other rooms. Maybe they were the sleeping quarters of the infected men they'd seen. Maybe one of the doors was the kitchen. James's stomach growled noisily. There might be food in there.

While Parker used the bathroom, James decided to peek in the other doors. The first room held supplies for the ship, such as ropes, life jackets, and tools. Two of the rooms contained metal bunkbeds, empty except for a few rumpled blankets strewn around the floor. There was a bloody hand print on the wall. Ugh. He didn't want to think about the men getting attacked and quickly shut the door.

As he was about to open the last door, Chen appeared at the bottom of the stairs, a handgun tucked into his waistband.

"Parker's in the bathroom. I'm waiting for him," James said.

"Good, good. He could use a friend right now," Chen said, thoughtfully, rubbing a hand down his stubbly whiskered chin. He opened the doors to the rooms with the beds, closing them quickly again.

Parker emerged from the bathroom just as Chen opened the door to the room James had hoped was the kitchen.

An infected man stumbled out, straight into Chen, wrapping his arms around him. James and Parker backed away as Chen struggled to get away from the zombie. Gnashing teeth gaped wide as the infected tried to bite Chen. They struggled for a few moments until Chen finally freed one arm enough to grab his gun and shoot the undead man. The zombie dropped to the ground.

"Go upstairs, boys," Chen growled over his shoulder.

They ran as fast as they could up the metal stairs. What would have happened if he or Parker had opened that door? He didn't even want to think about that.

Once they made it upstairs, Mom rushed over to him, grabbing his arm and looking around. "Did I hear a gunshot? Are you boys okay?"

"Yes, but we're fine, Mom. There was an infected man in one of the rooms down there. Luckily Chen took care of him," James said, but he had to admit he was a little shaken up. What if Chen hadn't come down there? They would have been infected for sure.

Dan rushed past them and hurried down the stairs. Hopefully that was the last zombie still on the boat.

[17]

"SOMEONE'S IN THE COTTAGE," Ava said, picking up Coco. The little dog growled low in his throat. For what seemed like the hundredth time, she whispered, "Quiet, Coco."

"Over there." Katie pointed to the stack of boxes on the side of the room and motioned for them to hide behind several of the larger ones. The door to the basement swung open just as Aiden ducked down. The soldiers marched quickly down the stairs.

"We've got to find those kids. We can't return without Ava, or the President will have our heads," one of the men said.

"Hey kids, you down here?" the other soldier called. "Come out, come out wherever you are."

Aiden held his breath. Any moment now Coco was going to bark, and it would all be over. He'd be captured and taken back to the scientists. A moan threatened to burst from his mouth. He hadn't experienced that kind of uncontrollable zombie moan since he'd been on the island. *Not now*, he thought as the soldiers moved closer to where they crouched behind the boxes.

Just then there *was* a moan, but Aiden was startled when it didn't come from him. It was an eerie, creepy, unearthly sound.

"What was that?" the soldier muttered.. He turned around in a circle.

"I don't know, but it's kind of freaking me out," the other man replied.

Aiden peeked through the boxes. The two soldiers stood right in front of him. A strange, glowing form seemed to float across the basement through the darkness. It hovered just above the soldiers' heads. The hairs on the back of Aiden's neck stood on end. He blinked several times and peered through the darkness again.

"Uh, Carter," one of the soldiers stuttered. "Let's get out of here."

"Yeah, we're done. Those kids aren't here."

The men ran up the basement steps and out of the cottage like they'd seen a ghost. Which maybe they had. Aiden had seen *something*. Whatever it was had gone now though. Maybe it had followed the soldiers out of the cottage. He glanced at Ava. Her eyes were huge as she turned to him.

"Oh my gosh. That Captain Bart!" she exclaimed.

"I told you this place was haunted," Katie said matter-of-factly.

"Dang. I couldn't even get a picture. My battery's dead," Ava sighed. "That would have been so cool."

A shiver ran down his back. It was suddenly kind of creepy in the basement. Had there really been a ghost down here? Aiden didn't know, but he suddenly wanted out of the basement. He wanted to explore the cottage above them. He'd never been inside a lighthouse. It would be pretty cool to see the view of the island from that high up.

"Come on," he said and climbed the stairs to the door.

"Oh my gosh, Aiden. Your speech is really getting better," Ava said as she climbed up after him. "Maybe if the scientists could see how much you've improved, it would change their minds."

Aiden shrugged. Wow, he was talking better now. He'd said those words without really thinking about it. He felt *almost* normal. He wanted to find a mirror and see if he looked more like the old Aiden. That would be amazing if the scientists really had found the cure. He didn't know what would happen to him now, only that he wanted to live. He hoped he would continue to recover while he was in hiding. Whatever medicines they had been giving him were working.

They tiptoed into the cottage store. Dust hung sparkling in the afternoon light that streamed through the windows. The front door was open, and glass glittered on the floor, thanks to the soldiers.

"Let's go up there," Aiden said, pointing to the door marked "Lighthouse." A grin spread across his face. He really could talk better now! The girls looked at him in surprise.

"Can you climb up all these stairs? There's about one hundred of them," Katie said.

"Yes, I think so," Aiden replied.

"You sound so normal. That's awesome, Aiden. Let's go check out the lighthouse," Ava said.

Climbing up the stairs wasn't too hard, and soon they were in the small, circular, glass room at the top. A large spotlight was placed in the center. It wasn't turned on right now, and Aiden wondered if it could be used without electricity. They probably had a generator somewhere.

"Look over there!" Ava exclaimed. "It's a boat, and it's heading this way,"

"The military won't let them near the island," Katie shrugged.

"Isn't that James and Cecily?" Aiden asked.

They watched as the boat drew closer. Soon they could read the words U.S. Coast Guard on the side of the vessel.

"It's got to be them," Ava cried, clapping. Coco barked, running in circles in the small space, Ava's excitement spreading to the little dog. "I hope they made it on the boat. I can't wait to meet your friends, Aiden," Ava said.

From their vantage point at the top of the light-house, they watched the boat cut through the waves until it finally began to slow. It came to a stop at the boathouse where Aiden had stayed. He wished he could see the people as they exited the boat, but they were too far away. Aiden sighed. Nothing had really changed, except that James and Cecily, Patty and Dan would be on the island.

He straightened up as a thought occurred to him. Maybe everything had changed! Surely Dan and Patty would protect him.

Running away had bought them some time, but maybe it was time to go back.

"Go back. See friends," Aiden said.

"Do you think it's safe now?" Ava asked.

Aiden nodded, and they looked at Katie.

"You should come with us. I won't let them take you off the island to a safe zone," Ava said. "I prom-ise. I'll talk to my dad."

Katie looked uncertain but finally nodded. "You don't know for sure that your friends are on the boat. We still have to be careful, Aiden. Let's get as close to the house as we can and see if it's them."

Aiden made his way down the stairs to the cottage below as fast as his legs would allow. Katie and Ava followed right behind him.

Once outside, they returned the way they had

come, still on the lookout for the soldiers. The sun was sinking quickly as night approached.

"Don't just rush in there, Aiden," Katie said. "We need to check it out first."

Aiden nodded, but he couldn't help the anticipation that shot through him. His friends *had* to be on that boat, he thought as he trudged alone. He wouldn't consider any other possibility.

[18]

JAMES STOOD on the deck and watched the waves as they crashed against the boat. They had been traveling for over an hour and he could finally see Cobb Island in the distance. He sagged against the railing in relief. Once they reached the safety of the island, everything would be okay. Aiden would be the cure the world so desperately needed, and everything could get back to normal. Of course, everything would also be different now too. People had suffered a lot, and many people had been infected with the virus. That was the bad part. The good part was he had some great friends and family around him, and that was what was really mattered. The video games and skateboards were fun and all, but those things just weren't important any more.

"We're almost there, man," Toby said, coming

across the deck to stand by James. Toby patted him on the back.

"Yeah, I'll be glad to finally get there. I wasn't sure if we'd make it," James replied.

"You're a good kid, James. I'm glad you're here with us."

James shrugged and muttered, "Thanks." But his heart swelled with something close to pride and happiness. It was a good feeling. "How much longer?" James asked.

"Less than ten minutes now. Dan radioed the island of our arrival. They are expecting us."

James nodded, turning back to gaze across the ocean. A dolphin appeared beside the boat. Then another dolphin joined the first. They leapt and frolicked in the waves. It was fun to watch them swimming alongside the boat. James smiled wryly. They had no idea what had happened to the humans. They just enjoyed being dolphins.

Cecily and Ella joined him on the deck, and they squealed in delight when they saw the dolphins playing in the water beside the boat.

"When we get to the island, I want to draw a picture of our boat with the dolphins," Cecily said.

"Me too," Ella said, always wanting to be included in Cecily's plans.

The boat slowed as they approached land. Brightly colored buildings dotted the shoreline. James could see a lighthouse in the distance.

"Let's gather up our belongings," Mom said from behind them. "We'll be at the island soon." She smiled brightly at James. Turning her face to the sun, she breathed in deeply. It was nice to see Mom happy.

Hurrying back inside, James pulled his backpack from a chair and sat down. There wasn't much to do really. They didn't have many things anymore. He decided that was okay.

Cecily plopped down in the chair beside him. She watched through the boat window at the passing town, its shops and homes giving off a relaxing, vacation feel.

"Do you think they'll give us our own house?"

"I don't know. I'll just be happy to see how Aiden is doing," James said.

Ella sat on the other side of James, pulling her legs crisscross underneath her. She clutched Mopsy, her toy bunny close, but she smiled at James. "I miss Aiden, too," she said.

Mom sat down across from them, her Bug Out Bag at her feet. "I know you're excited to see Aiden again, but remember he's going through a lot of testing with the scientists right now. He might not be in the same place on the island, or he might be really busy. I'm sure you'll get a chance to talk to him soon, okay? I just don't want you to be disappointed if he's not available right away.

"Sure, I understand," James said, nodding. He hoped Aiden was doing better. He deserved that.

The boat slowly pulled alongside the dock. Toby and John jumped onto the wooden dock. It was small for such a large vessel, but they managed to secure the boat. James glanced up the sloping lawn to the large, white house. A knot formed in his belly as several men in black uniforms, rifles in their hands, rushed down the hill to meet them. Their group had finally arrived on Cobb Island, but James suddenly wondered if they were really welcome.

[19]

AIDEN CROUCHED behind the trees next to the house. Katie and Ava knelt next to him. They scanned the area but couldn't see any movement. The boat was tied to the dock, and it rocked in the water, hitting the wood with a gentle thud every few moments.

The sun hung low over the horizon now, and it would be dark soon. Aiden's stomach growled loudly. He was hungry, but he didn't have time to think about food right now. He wanted to see who had been on the boat.

"I used to be able to sneak into the house, but I don't think it's a good idea now with all the soldiers around," Katie whispered.

"Look in the window," Aiden whispered back.

"I'll go," Ava said,

"You better stay with Aiden. You don't want to get caught," Katie said.

Aiden shook his head. He needed to see for himself if James and Cecily had made it to the island.

Katie shrugged and nodded.

"I'm coming too," Ava said. Coco lay at her feet. It didn't look like the little dog wanted to go anywhere.

A door opened at the front of the house, and Chen Wu stepped out onto the porch.

Aiden sucked in a breath. He hadn't seen what had happened to Chen when they had fought off the zombies at the Masterson Pharmaceuticals building. He'd thought the infected had gotten to him, but he was wrong. Fear crept up the back of his neck, and he shivered. Chen wasn't a good guy, no matter how much he pretended to be. Chen must have been on that boat.

Aiden realized that James and the others didn't know Chen had been with Frank that night. He watched as Chen crossed the sloping lawn towards the boathouse. He would walk right by them. Aiden crouched lower. Ava and Katie did the same. When Chen got closer, Aiden noticed a bandage on his arm. His shirt was wet with sweat, and he stumbled as he walked past.

Was Chen infected? It looked like it to Aiden. He couldn't be sure though.

Chen stopped at the door to the boathouse. Glancing around as if making sure no one was watching, he slipped a key into the door and slipped inside.

"Who is that?" Katie whispered.

"Yeah, and why is he going in the boathouse?" Ava whispered. "My dad said only the scientists were allowed in there."

"Chen. Come on," Aiden answered, motioning toward the boathouse.

Ava picked up the tired Coco, and crouching down, they ran to the back of the boathouse. Aiden peeked in the window. It was getting dark in the room, but he could see Chen rummaging through drawers and cabinets. What was he looking for?

"He's bleeding," Ava whispered.

Aiden nodded. Blood had seeped through the bandage on Chen's arm. It could be a knife wound or something, but it looked like he was infected to Aiden. If Chen turned into a zombie, he would endanger everyone on the island.

Chen pulled out several small bottles, glancing at the labels and discarding them. *He's looking for the cure,* Aiden realized. *He's going to steal it for himself.*

This was almost the same thing that had happened before, except now Chen wanted the cure for himself. If he stole the vaccine, did the scientists have more? Aiden didn't know. The formula that had worked on Aiden had been the last one they'd tried. It was the one in the boathouse. The scientists didn't know how much he was improving yet. Would it make a difference to their plans?

Chen found a needle and syringe. He was going to

inject himself with the vaccine. Aiden had guessed correctly. Chen was infected.

The door to the boathouse flung open, and Chen whirled around as James, Cecily, and Parker entered the room. Aiden shook his head. He didn't expect to see Chen or Parker on the island. Today was full of surprises.

"What are you doing in here?" James said.

Cecily ran past James and glanced quickly around the room. "They said Aiden and Ava have disappeared. If they ran away, they must have had a good reason," she said.

Aiden had seen enough. James and Cecily were on the island. They could turn themselves in now. Aiden had people who would fight for him now. Ava and Katie, of course, and his dad, but he also had all the people from Ashland.

"Come on," Aiden said. He squared his shoulders and walked as quickly as he could around the boathouse to the front door. They burst inside just as Chen pulled a gun from his pocket and pointed it at James and Cecily.

"Don't come any closer," Chen said, his hand shaking.

The virus was coursing through his body, and he could turn at any moment, Aiden thought.

Chen glanced around in shock at Aiden, Ava, and Katie as they entered the room. There were six kids in the boathouse standing in front of Chen, their hands above their heads in the gesture of surrender. Six kids who knew that he had been infected and was trying to steal the cure.

James glanced over at Aiden, taking in the girls and the dog. He nodded quickly then focused back on Chen. Cecily darted over to Aiden and hugged him tightly.

"You kids stay right where you are," Chen wheezed, his breaths coming in hollow gasps. "Come over here, Parker." Chen motioned with the gun for Parker to cross the room and stand beside him.

Parker hesitated for a split second before stepping closer to James. "No. I don't think I'm going along with you this time."

Chen shrugged. "Doesn't matter, I guess. One of the zombies bit me as I fought with it on the boat. If the military found out I was infected, they would never let me on the island. I need this," he said, clutching the small bottle of medicine with his free hand.

"We can get you help. You don't have to do this alone," James said.

Chen shook his head and glanced wildly around the room. Then he gasped and dropped to his knees. The gun fell from his hand. Chen teetered there for a moment before sprawling across the floor.

[20]

JAMES STARED in disbelief at Chen where he lay on the floor. Would he really have shot them all to steal the vaccine? Desperate people could do anything if they thought it would save themselves. Chen was in a bad way too.

James knelt beside him and touched his neck. His pulse was weak, but he was still alive. Chen opened bloodshot eyes and stared at James.

"What should we do?" James asked, glancing at Aiden.

"I'll go get help," the younger girl said and ran out of the boathouse carrying the dog.

"We don't have much time," Aiden said. "Give him the vaccine now."

James stared at Aiden in shock. He couldn't believe it. Aiden had just spoken clearly. And not just a word but a whole sentence. He wasn't sure what to do. Should he give Chen the medicine? He didn't know how to give someone a shot anyway.

The other girl pushing James out of the way. She pried the small bottle out of Chen's clenched fist.

"What are you doing?" James asked, eyeing the dark-haired girl curiously.

The girl rolled up Chen's shirt sleeve. Who was she?

"Can you give yourself the shot?" the girl asked Chen, ignoring James.

Chen nodded weakly.

James searched a few drawers until he found an alcohol wipe. He cleaned a spot on Chen's arm.

"I'm Katie, by the way," she said.

James nodded. "I'm James," he replied.

He held Chen's trembling arm as still as possible. Katie attached the needle to the syringe and handed it to Chen. With a shaking hand, Chen plunged the syringe into his arm. When he was finished, he fell back against the hard wood floor.

Parker knelt beside James and gazed at Chen. Parker's face was so sad that James swallowed down a lump in his throat. Chen had been a friend to Parker after his dad had died. If Chen didn't make it, Parker would have one more person to mourn. There was nothing more they could do. They had to wait and hope the medicine worked. James sighed. Hopefully the vaccine was really the cure and they got the medicine to Chen in time.

Cecily sat on the floor beside Parker. She slipped her hand into his and squeezed. Parker tensed for a moment, but he didn't pull away.

The door burst open, and the room filled with people. Dr. Winters ran in first and clasped Aiden to him in a fierce hug. Dan, John, Toby, and Mom entered, followed by two other scientists. Admiral Walker and three soldiers entered last. Their guns were loaded and ready.

"What happened?" Dr. Winters asked Aiden.

"Chen was infected. We gave him medicine," Aiden said.

Dr. Winters's eyes widened at Aiden's clear speech. He smiled, pulling Aiden close and hugging him tightly. "Good job, son. But why did you run away?" Dr. Winters asked.

"I can tell you why they ran," Katie said, standing up and facing the room. "The scientists wanted to kill Aiden and study his body. They were going to do it without your knowledge, Dr. Winters. Aiden found out about their plan and decided he better not wait to see what would happen." Katie planted her hands on her hips. "So what are you going to do about it?"

"I would never have allowed that to happen!" Dr. Winters exclaimed. "I'm sorry you didn't confide in me, son."

Ava and the President entered the boathouse. James hadn't had the chance to do more than put his bag in his room before they heard that Aiden and Ava were missing. He and Cecily had gone down to the boathouse to look for clues. That's when they'd found Chen. James shook his head and glanced at where Chen lay on the floor. Dr. Winters took charge then and ordered Chen to be placed on the cot. More drugs were administered. The scientists gathered around Chen, eager to test the vaccine on another subject.

"It's a bit crowded in here," the President said in his most authoritative voice. "Let's take this discussion up to the house. I want to know who is responsible for causing my daughter such distress that she ran away."

Everyone exited the boathouse and strode up the hill to the big, white house. James glanced at Aiden, who looked better than James had ever seen him. The vaccine the scientists had been giving Aiden just might be the cure. James couldn't wait to hear the whole story.

[21]

AIDEN SAT in a chair facing the group. He'd been introduced to a lot of people from Richmond and the CDC. He was relieved to see they'd made it here safely. He cleared his throat and began to speak in a soft but clear voice. He nodded toward Dr. Benton.

"Like Katie said, Ava and I overheard Dr. Benton talking to another scientist about performing an autopsy on me. He said it didn't matter what my dad said because it would be done before he could stop them. That was why we ran away,"

Dr. Basheer, Dr. Takahashi, and Dr. Benton looked around nervously.

Dad jumped up and paced the floor, his hands balled into fists like he might punch someone. Aiden had never seen him so mad. Dad glared at the scientists. "I can't believe you would even consider something like that. And to go behind my back!"

Dr. Benton looked at the floor, his face slowly turning red.

"If scientists weren't so difficult to find at the moment, I'd fire you immediately!" President Harrison said, his brows drawn together in a line.

Ava slipped her hand into her dad's and smiled up at him, a look of innocence on her face as if the whole island hadn't been looking for her. "I took lots of photos along the way, Daddy. I'll add them to my social media accounts as soon as I'm able. It's going to be amazing," Ava said, grinning at Aiden.

Aiden looked at his feet so she wouldn't see him roll his eyes.

"Katie helped us a lot. She should stay here from now on," Ava added.

"This is *my* house after all," Katie said, crossing her arms.

"Yes, of course you will stay here under our protection," President Harrison agreed.

"Will you find my parents and bring them back here?" Katie said, lifting her chin defiantly. The President nodded quickly, motioning to several soldiers.

"Of course, I'll send a team to find them right away."

After the soldiers left the room, he continued, "Based on what the scientists have told me, I'm confident we have found the cure we have been searching for. They are watching Chen closely to see how he responds to the vaccine. If all goes well, we will begin manufacturing the medication and shipping it around the United States."

"You'll share the formula with the *entire* world, for free, right?" James asked.

The President hesitated.

"Daddy!" Ava exclaimed, stomping her foot.

"Yes. Of course. The XR-30 vaccine belongs to the entire world," the President agreed, finally.

Everyone began talking at once, the excitement and relief evident on their faces.

Aiden glanced around the room. James, Katie, and Parker were talking quietly. Parker seemed like a different boy than the one he'd known before, Aiden thought in amazement. Ava and Cecily knelt on the floor, playing with Cupcake and Coco. Ella sat by Patty on the sofa, holding onto Mopsy, the stuffed bunny she'd tried to give to him on several occasions. Dan stood next to Patty, his arm around her as he discussed something with John.

Grandma Wilma held baby Rose, and the little boys ran around the room, playing with their plastic dinosaurs and making roaring noises.

"I need to document this moment," Ava declared. She motioned for everyone to gather around Aiden. James, Cecily, Katie and Parker squeezed in close to his side. Ava pulled Ella in next to her and positioned them in front of the group. After making sure everyone could be seen, Ava snapped the photo. Aiden sighed.

His mom would be happy if she could see them all now. A peaceful feeling flowed through him and he smiled. *I made it, Mom. I'm alive.*

ACKNOWLEDGMENTS

A huge thank you to my family for supporting me in my writing journey, especially my daughter Nina and my husband Ross. Thank you to my editor Jeni Chappelle and my talented cover designer Daqri Bernardo. Thank you to all the readers who have loved these characters as much as I have. Your support means the world to me. I love you all!